JUGAADU

Aditya Mishra

Invincible Publishers

First published in India in 2018

ISBN: 978-93-87328-59-4

Invincible Publishers

G-120, Sushant Lok III, Sector 57, Gurgaon-122002

Registered Address: Opposite Kasturba Ashram, Radaur, Haryana - 135133

Dedicated to my Maa…

Acknowledgement

This work would not have been possible without my Editor, Ms. Aditi Saxena, for turning my dream into reality, and my designer, Ms. Ruchika Khanna, who sincerely eased my burden of designing the book cover.

I express my sincere gratitude to my friends, the list of whom is so long that I can't name them all here, for all the vivid life experiences which we shared together, and my family for all their support and for giving me the peace to start something new in my life.

A big thanks to my school teachers who tolerated all our mischiefs and naughty behaviour.

CHAPTER ONE

'Lucknow Montessori School welcomes all the freshers to the School', said a board at the main entrance gate of the school. It was the first day of school after the vacations. The junior students were very happy to be returning back to school after the long summer vacations.

There were many new faces also to be seen that morning. After 10th standard's board exams, many students left the school to go to other schools, depending upon their interests in some particular subjects, while many new students from different other school applied to LMS (it being the most reputed school in Lucknow, the city of Nawabs).

Among all the fresh faces at school, was a decent looking guy, fair in complexion, curly hair, well dressed in a grey trouser and a white shirt, and wearing flashy white frames. He was newly admitted to the school and was carrying his school bag with a tag 'Shiv Shantanu Yadav'.

He went to the reception where a few peons were chit-chatting, and said, "Good Morning, Sir. I am a new admission to the school. Would you please tell me which class I have been assigned to and the way to it?"

A very old man with lot of tobacco in his mouth, who was sitting at the reception replied in his heavy voice, "Which standard?"

Shiv said, "XI standard."

The old man gave him a piercing look again and said, “How much did you scored in X standard?”

“86%”

He seemed quite shocked at this and replied, “It’s strange. The management doesn’t takes new students with less than 90% score. Well, whatever it may be, you check your fee receipt, your section should be written over there.”

Shiv took out the receipt from his wallet and found that it was written 11-D on it. “Sir, where is 11-D?” he asked.

“It’s on the second floor.”

“Thank you.”

Entering the school premises, Shiv found the school to be quite small in area, particularly in comparison with his previous school which was a boarding in Nainital, with a total area of more than 72 hectares. It was thus quite natural for him to have found this school with only 10 hectares of area quite small in size.

He started climbing the staircase to first floor, where there were washbasins with ‘DRINKING WATER’ written over them. On his left was a cabin belonging to one ‘Neeraj Kapoor’. Beneath the name, his designation as the ‘Coordinator - Class 11 & 12’ was also written. Shiv understood that this was the guy he had to be careful of as long as he stayed in that school.

There was a hallway right in front of Neeraj’s cabin, which read 12 sections. To his right was the Physics laboratory which ended nearly 40 metres ahead, beyond which was a staircase.

Shiv moved up to the 2nd floor where he saw a board with 11-C on it. Behind it were 11-D and then 11-G. ‘Where are the other sections A, B, E and F?’ was the first question that struck Shiv’s mind, but he ignored it and went toward his section.

• • •

There already were some students present in the class, but it hadn't gotten crowded yet. The time was 7:30 AM by his watch, which left thirty minutes before the official school routines started. He expected the other students to arrive in the meantime.

Always being before time was a quality that Shiv possessed, as boarders are usually quite punctual of time. He entered the class and found were two cupboards and a blackboard on his right. The blackboard was at the centre of the wall, with one cupboard on either side of it. Shiv found an empty seat in a corner on the right. He put his bag on the desk and sat on his seat.

It was 7:55 AM by then and the class had started to become a mess with lots of boys and girls. After a while, a girl wearing a red coloured 'PREFECT' batch came into the class and shouted, "Everyone! Empty out the class and gather at the auditorium for the assembly." She then moved forward, perhaps to empty out the other class-rooms.

Everyone started pulling out their diaries from their bags and walked out of the class. Shiv noticed that the students had covered their diaries with different colour'd papers; some were green, some red, some yellow and some blue.

These colours represented the different houses that the students were divided into: red house, blue house, green house and yellow house. He didn't have a diary, so he simply made his way to the assembly. He was used to such assemblies, having experienced similar ones in Nainital.

The principal welcomed the students back after the holidays. Some singing and morning prayers were conducted as part of the Assembly, after which, the Head Boy of the School took the pledge, "India is my country…bla bla bla bla."

After the morning assembly, all the students started to move back to their respective classes. The prefects were checking students' shoes, dress and deportment, etc. Shiv, being properly dressed, wasn't sent out of the line and went quietly back to his class.

On reaching the class, Shiv went back to his seat and sat down. A tall/geeky kind of a guy came and sat beside him.

"Hey, I am Prateek Rai. I think you are new to this school."

"Hey, I am Shiv. Yes, you are right. I am new in this place."

Prateek had scored 92% in his 10th standard board exams (Well, that's a lot of marks), yet the boy was sad for not making it to the best section.

He told Shiv that all the guys/girls with a percentage above 95% made it to the best section, i.e. 11-E.

Then came in the class teacher, Mr. Anurag Singh, who was also the chemistry teacher there. Anurag was a short, fat man with little hair on his head. He must have done some chemical reaction on himself, Shiv thought.

Shiv was thankful to have Prateek on his side, as he filled him in on everyone at the school. He told him that Anurag Singh was the Chemistry boss at the school and was the best available teacher for chemistry in the whole of Lucknow.

Anurag sir took out his attendance register and started calling out the names of students. After the attendance, he left for his class and said that he would visit again before the last bell.

Their first lecture was that of Environmental Sciences. Prateek was unaware of its teacher himself, as it was a new subject and new teacher had been assigned for it. He, along with the other old students, had been transferred from the seniors' building to the senior secondary building for the first time.

An attractive figure entered the class just then. Their new teacher was a lady with above average height and a very fair complexion. Much to the disappointment of Shiv, a mark of sindoor showed clearly on her forehead, a sign of her being married.

She was wearing a green saree and looked fabulous in it. Everybody stood up and wished her in a sing-song 'Good Morning, Ma'am'.

"Good morning, students. How are you all?"

"Great ma'am," all the students replied in a chorus.

"This is my first interaction with all of you. Whether you are new or old, I have never taught the junior section, so I am completely new to you all and you all are new to me too. As it is the first class, I don't wish to start teaching just yet. Let's start with an introduction session today. I am Preeti Tandon and I will be teaching you Environment Science."

The students then started introducing themselves from the right-most side. They started telling their name, the percentage of marks they had obtained in X standard, the last school they attended and their hobbies.

The first one to introduce himself was a thin guy who said, "My name is Mudit Sinha. I did my tenth from the same school. I scored 93.75% in my X Boards. My hobbies are cricket, football, music and riding my bike."

The session then started where each student stood up at his/her seat and introduced themselves. After some time, Shiv's turn came. He stood up and said, "My name is Shiv Shantanu Yadav. I scored 86% in the tenth boards, I..."

Shiv was surprised to see that each and every student present in the class had turned around to look at him, as if he had stolen something or a bomb had exploded in the class.

Shiv finished his introduction nonetheless. "I did my X from Snow Hill Boarding School, Nainital. I like to play Basketball and Football". He sat back on his seat.

• • •

"Why was everyone looking at me after I told my marks?" Shiv asked Prateek.

"Actually, the school doesn't accept new admissions for class XI with less than 90% in X Boards, that's why. It is just unusual, that's it. Nothing to worry about, bud."

No lectures took place that day, as most classes were spent in making introductions to the teachers. Shiv noticed a strange thing about his class that there was hardly a student there with less than a score of 91%. The highest percentage scorer in the class was Mudit Sinha with his 93.75%, so he was made the boys' monitor of the class.

The other monitor was a fair girl named Saumya Singh. She was about 5'3'' in height, with short hair that only came down to her neck, and quite healthy in stature.

There were a total of 41 students in his class, out of which, 12 were girls and the rest were guys.

The rest of his subjects were: Mathematics taught by Mr. Rajan Pandey, Chemistry by Mr. A N Singh, Physics by Mr. Neeraj Kapoor, the coordinator, English literature by Mrs. Kavita Srivastava, and English Language by Dr. Mrs. Zaidi.

This was the data that he collected from Prateek, as he hadn't yet had an interaction with any of the teachers.

When the school hours were over, he bid goodbye to Prateek and came down the stairs from the second floor.

The feeling which one gets while coming out of the school after 'chhutti' is that of such relief, a breath of fresh air after the boring lectures by boring teachers, trying to explaining all the physics, chemistry and biology.

As Shiv came out of the school, he found his driver waiting for him outside. As soon as the driver spotted him, he came rushing towards him and said, "Chhote bhaiya! Give me your bag. You must be tired from carrying this all day."

"Oh, it is not that heavy, Rakesh."

Shiv boarded the Scorpio which had been sent to pick him up. His house was in Indranagar, which was about 8-10 kilometres away from his school in Gomtinagar. During the entire ride back, the driver showed him around the city of Lucknow.

As Shiv was new to Lucknow, the driver showed him the Polytechnic Chowraha, Wave Mall, Munshi Pulia Chowraha, etc. Shiv, however, didn't seem to be enjoying the scenery or anything else at all. He was too busy in his own thoughts.

No classes had been held that day as it was the first day of the session, so Shiv couldn't exactly get an idea of how his new school worked, but he had heard a lot about the place from his parents and family friends.

According to everyone, this was the finest school in the city and all the Who's Who of Lucknow sent their children to this school for a better experience.

According to Shiv's dad, if he got thrown out of this school too (Oops, did I say thrown out? Oh, sorry. Everyone has a past and so does Shiv, which he doesn't want to disclose just yet), he'd have no future and he wouldn't be able to do anything with his life.

Only time could tell what the future had in store for Shiv. He reached home and was determined to leave everything upto God and cheer himself up, as he was in a new city where he was going to have new friends and a new kind of fun.

***

On the next day at school, Shiv underwent the same morning routine as the day before, complete with the morning assembly, the uniform check up, the pledge and the daily prayers, etc.

Mudit (the new monitor) escorted the line back to their class. As soon as Shiv entered his class, he saw some strange faces in the class, who had not been in the line, nor were they present during the Assembly.

They were 4-5 guys there. They were not in proper uniform. One of them was wearing golden coloured specs. He was an average height'd guy with a normal complexion and very silky hair parted from one side. He looked decent. His friend was fat guy with short hair, wearing a thick gold chain around his neck, which must weigh about half a kg or so. He himself must have weighed more than 90 kilograms. He looked like a rich spoilt brat and was narrating some story of a vacation at some hill station to the rest of the guys. All of them were taking a lot of interest in it.

Shiv entered the class, went over to his seat, and took out a register for the next lecture. Prateek came to sit beside him. Shiv asked him, "I didn't see those guys at the Assembly. Who are they?"

"Oh! Those guys? They are the most BHOKALI gang of the school. You see that guy with the golden frames? His name is Devvrat Dixit, but everyone calls him Dev."

"Okay, and that fat one?"

"That guy with the thick gold chain is Mustafa. Everyone knows them at school. They never attend the Assembly, sneak in and out of school all the time and fight with the other guys over petty issues. They are upto no good, but still they keep the class alive. It is really fun to be in their presence. Shh...Anurag sir is here."

Shiv turned to look at the door and saw Anurag sir standing there with an attendance register in his hand. Everyone stood up at their seat and wished him, "GOOOOOOOOD MOOOORNING, Sir."

"Good Morning, students. Sit down."

• • •

Dev stood up on his seat, took out a packet from his bag, called Mustafa along and went up to the Teacher's table.

"Guruji! Mithai."

"Mithai! For what?"

"Guruji, Mustafa and I both passed the class X board exams. That's why."

"Oho, congratulations! I will just have one, the rest you can distribute in the class. By the way, how much did you two score?"

Mustafa replied happily, "Sir, I got 62% and Dev got 63%."

"Okay, that is not so good, but i am sure you both will get more than 85% next time."

"Oho! come on, Sir. We have just ended with one board exams. Why should we worry about the next one just yet? We still have two years to worry about them."

The whole class started laughing at once, and it was quite visible from Anurag sir's face that he was not expecting such an answer from Mustafa.

He gave an angry look to Mustafa, but he showed no sign of shame. Instead, he started laughing and said, "Arrey, pakka sir. Of course we will score more than 85%, sir."

Meanwhile, Dev asked Mudit to distribute the sweets to all the classmates as Anurag sir started taking attendance.

Dev and Mustafa were back to their seats at the end of the middle row.

Shiv had a question in his mind. He asked Prateek, "Hey Prateek, how come Dev and Mustafa are in this school despite such low percentages, when you said that the school doesn't keep anyone below 90%?"

"I think you know the answer, Shiv. It is the same way that you are here in this school. There is a lot of politics in here, bud. Dev's father is the DM of the city, and Mustafa's elder brother has some connection with the founder. Plus, his father owns the biggest real estate business in Lucknow. I am damn sure that you too have been admitted to the school through some such connection, man."

"I don't think so, Prateek. I don't have any connections in this school, neither do I have any such big government officers in my family."

"Is that so? Achcha tell me, what do your father and mother do?"

"My father is an MLA and my mom is a housewife."

"Oho, here comes another one! Your father is an MLA. Do you think he is an ordinary man? Do you really think that he doesn't have his own connections? Listen dude, an MLA in not an ordinary man in Lucknow. Welcome to Lucknow, bro. This is the place where you will see most cars with either a red or a blue beacon on them. If you know someone who's at a high post or authority, things will go very easily for you. Otherwise, life is not that easy in The City Of Nawabs, bud!"

He has said all of this in one breath. As Shiv was new to Lucknow, he had not seen much of the shades of the city.

The next lecture was that of English Language. Their teacher, Dr. Zaidi, was an elderly lady, short height'd, with thick glasses in silver coloured frames, and strictly professional. She started with one of the favourite topics of grammar teachers - NOUN. She gave an introduction of Nouns and Pronouns, and then gave some assignments as homework.

Next was the lecture of Maths. Rajan sir entered the class, he was a medium height'd man, wearing thin golden framed specs. He seemed to have put a lot of oil on his head.

He was the best mathematics teacher for the senior sections at their school, according to Prateek. He started the class with algebra. The other guys in class, Dev and all, were enjoying themselves at the back benches of the middle row. Shiv noticed they didn't even have a register, nor were they noting anything down from the lecture. After this lecture, they had their lunch break.

"So students, you have to do Exercises 1.3, 4 and 5, and bring it to the next lecture."

"Thank you, sir."

***

Most of the students took out their lunch boxes and went out of the class. Dev and the gang were amongst the first ones to move out of the class. All the students were interacting with their friends from the other sections.

Shiv went out of the class as Prateek too went to see his friends from other sections. They had all been divided according to their marks.

Shiv was alone, so he went downstairs and proceeded to the canteen area. There he saw Dev and the gang bullying some other guy. Shiv was thinking of naming them the D Company.

Shiv bought an Appy Fizz from the canteen and went back to his class. He opened his lunch box and found sandwiches inside. He started having his lunch. He didn't have much appetite, but still he had to finish the contents of his lunch box.

The D Company entered the class after some time. They sat on top of the benches. Suddenly, Dev bent down and put something to his ears. Shiv noticed that it was a mobile. Dev answered his call and noticed Shiv watching him using his mobile.

Before Shiv could remember whether mobile phones was allowed inside the school, Dev rushed to his desk and said,

"Hey! Whoever you are, you didn't see anything and you are not going to tell anyone about anything. Is that understood?"

"Of course, bro. I didn't see any mobile and I am not going to tell anyone about any mobile."

Mustafa shouted, "Hey Dev, stop bullying that guy. Some teacher is coming this way."

Dev replied, "Coming! So you get it, new boy. Keep your mouth shut." He then went back to his friends.

So it was clear to Shiv that a mobile phone was definitely not allowed inside the school, yet these guys did it.

Before he could think of anything else, their English Literature teacher entered the classroom. She was a stout lady, short height'd again. This was the only teacher, Shiv noticed, who did not wear any specs.

"GOOOOOD AAAAFTERNOOOOON, MA'AM!" said all the students in unison.

"Good afternoon, students. Sit down, please."

All the students started taking out fresh registers and books from their bag. The back benchers started shouting, "Ma'am, introduction please!"

At the humble request of all the students (who were just in the mood to pass the time through an introduction session), she replied, "Well, my name is Kavita Srivastava and I am your new teacher for English Literature. I will be taking the book 'Pygmalion' by George Bernard Shaw. Apart from that, I too am a new recruit to the school, so you all must know more about the school than I do. Now, I would like you all to introduce yourselves. Let's start from the back benchers."

The first one to start was Mustafa. "Ma'am, my name is Mustafa Khan. I got 62% in my X board exams. I am an old student from this school and my friends call me Khan, only

KHAN." This made the rest of the students laugh. (They just needed a topic to laugh at.)

Second was Dev. "Ma'am, my name is Devvrat Dixit. I scored 63% in my X board exams and I am also an old student of the school. My friends call me Dev, only DEV," he said, reiterating the Khan style.

Then, it was Mohit's turn. He was an extremely fair and cute looking guy. "Ma'am, my name is Mohit Chopra. I scored 88% in my X board exams and I am also an old student from this school," Mohit said and sat back in his seat.

On seeing Mohit sitting back, Dev said, "Bhai, this is cheating."

Kavita ma'am said, "What is cheating, Dev?"

Dev said, "Ma'am, it was decided that everyone would also tell their nicknames as part of the introduction. Mohit! Come on, be a man."

Mohit said, "Ma'am, my friends call me chikna, Mohit CHIKNA."

Everyone started laughing at this reply. Even Kavita ma'am started laughing and asked, "Why do your friends call you Chikna?"

"Ma'am, I don't know. They just do."

Everyone started laughing again.

Then it came the turn of Prashant. He was an average height'd, fair guy with a muscular built. "Ma'am, my name is Prashant Tiwari. I scored 82% in my X boards. I am also an old student of this school. The gang calls me Binnu, because that's my pet name at home. Everyone in my colony calls me Binnu too."

The lecture was over with just the introduction session again. The next lecture was that of Chemistry, but Anurag sir had left for some other branch due to an emergency. Students were thus asked to leave for their homes, as it was the last lecture.

• • •

CHAPTER TWO

The first week of school was neither too tiring nor hectic for Shiv. Nothing extra-ordinary or important happened in school in the first week, as most of the time was spent in introductions or just the initial lessons of the subject.

The second week started with the coordinator, Neeraj Kapoor, entering the class and saying, "Anurag sir is on leave for a week, so he won't be coming to school. Class monitor, please mark the attendance in the first lecture, get it signed by me and submit it to the Vice Principal ma'am." To this, Mudit (our class monitor) replied, "Sure, sir."

Binnu: "What happened to mota(Anurag sir)?"

Chikna: "I think he lost his motion."

Khan: "Oh ho, whatever it is, look at the bigger picture! No chemistry classes for a week. Let's plan something out."

Chikna: "No man, I didn't get 90% in my X boards, but I will get it in XI. Or else, my father is going to throw me out of the house."

Dev: "Oye, come on, chikne. Khan is right. Listen guys, let's have as much as fun we can now. From next week, we have five lectures each of Chemistry and Environmental studies, then maths and physics on alternate days, and a lecture daily for English Language and English Literature. There is nothing to study in the Environment subject."

Khan: "There is no class for Chemistry, English Language and Literature we will study right before the exams, the Physics lecture will have a revision of class X, and Maths we will study from NEXT WEEK. Saturday is off anyway."

Chikna: "So?"

Khan: "So, shall we go to Deva Shareef tomorrow?"

Dev: "Done."

Binnu: "Done."

Chikna: "Yaar, pakka we will study from next week na?"

Dev: "Oho, it's for sure, my dear."

Chikna: "Okay then, done."

Dev: "Four guys, two bikes, Deva Shareef, done."

On one side, the D Company was planning their week, while Shiv had other plans on his side.

"Hey, Shiv! Which book are you referring to for Maths?" The studious Prateek asked Shiv.

"First, I'll study from the M.L. Agrawal book prescribed by the school, then I shall try doing some problems from R.S. Agrawal too."

"R.S. Agrawal? That's a good book. I have seen students prepare for IIT JEE using that same book."

"Yeah, my father told me to study from that book."

"By the way, Shiv, which coaching are you going to?"

"Coaching! What for?"

"For PCM. What else?"

"I don't go to any coaching, I study at home."

"Okay, but you will have to join a coaching."

"Why?"

"You see, all the teachers who teach at our school here, have their own private coaching centres for extra money. I have even heard that they are partial towards students who attend those classes. They give full marks in the practical exams to those who go to their coaching centres."

"Oho, I didn't know this, yaar. Thanks for keeping me updated."

"Anytime, bud."

During his way back, Shiv kept thinking of what Prateek had said. He had been shocked.

He had not thought like that. Perhaps, Prateek did not know much, Shiv thought, as he had also just heard those things. Yet, what if all those things were true? Shiv dismissed the thought for the moment.

He started looking out the window of his car. The students were all going to their respective houses. Some younger kids were on their rickshaws, while the older ones were on their bicycles, making their way home in groups of four or five.

Girls were going home in their rickshaws and school vans too. Dev was sitting on his black Pulsar 220 DTS-Fi parked on the roadside. Wait a second, did he really see Dev? Oh yes, it was indeed Dev sitting on his bike at the roadside.

Shiv stopped his car and popped his head out of the window. "Hi Dev, sitting alone? Is there a problem?"

"Hey! Hi, new boy. Yeah, I think there is some problem with my bike. It's not starting. I checked as thoroughly as I could. There seems to be some engine breakdown."

"It seems like a new bike, yaar."

"Yeah, it's a new one. I got it after my X board results."

"Where do you live, dude?"

"Ah well, I live in Indranagar - B block, and you?"

"Hey, I live in Indranagar too. My house is near the picnic spot road, Kukrail."

"Okay, that's great, yaar!"

"Come, man. I will drop you, it'll be on the way."

"Oh, that's so kind of you. Thank you so much."

"Rakesh! Do me a favour. Take his bike to a mechanic, get the problem sorted and bring it back home," Shiv said to his driver.

"But bhaiya ji, are you going to drive home alone? You don't even have a driving licence."

"Arrey baba, don't worry about that at all," Dev interrupted.

"Okay, bhaiya ji. I will return home after repairing this bike"

"Hey, Rakesh. Keep this 1000 rupees for the repairing and let me know if it costs more. I have only 1000 with me right now. I will give you the rest, if required, when you come back," Dev said and offered Rakesh the thousand rupee note, which he took.

"Come, Dev. Have a seat."

Shiv took the driver's seat, while Dev sat next to him. Within seconds, they were on their way back home. He drove at a speed not more than 40 kmph.

"Hey, new boy. Do you mind if I light a cigarette?"

"First of all, my name is Shiv. And second, no I won't mind if you smoke. By the way, which brand do you smoke?"

"I smoke Classic Mild. Do you want one?"

"No bro, I don't smoke."

"Oh, that's great. Have you never had even a single puff?"

"No bro, I haven't tried it yet."

"Okay, I won't force you for it."

Shiv opened his window a little to let the smoke pass out.

"I don't think your bike will get repaired today. Shall I pick you up tomorrow for school?" Shiv asked.

"I was thinking the same too, but I will not be going to school tomorrow."

"Oh, don't worry about the bike, man. You can't miss school just because your bike broke down. I will come pick you up, buddy."

"Oh, no no no Shiv. Thank you so much for being so helpful, but tomorrow we are all leaving from school in the morning to go to Deva Shareef, and will return before the classes get over."

"Oh, so you guys are planning to bunk tomorrow?"

"Yeah, bunk."

"By the way, what is Deva Shareef?"

"It is a famous dargaah about 40 kms from the Polytechnic Chowraha. It is a popular tourist place. Why don't you come along with us?"

"Me! Are you sure?"

"Yes, of course I am sure. It'll be fun. Come on, we will have a lot of fun."

"Tomorrow, hmm…okay, done. So, I will pick you up tomorrow from your house."

"Yes, give me your number."

They both exchanged their numbers

"Hey man, that's my house on the opposite side."

"The one with the huge black gates?"

"Yeah, just drop me here."

"Okay then, see you tomorrow. Bye."

"Bye. See ya."

***

Shiv had promised Dev about going to Deva Shareef with his group, but he was still not sure whether bunking classes at the new school was such a good idea. Since he had now promised Dev, he felt that he had to follow through with it.

The only thing he could do now was hope that the plan got cancelled somehow. However, it had to be done one day, since he hadn't been to any new place in this City of Nawabs, and it could prove to be a memorable journey too. With all these troubling thoughts in his mind, Shiv sat atop his toilet seat, which was his favourite place to think. He was deep in his thoughts, what would he tell Rakesh? If Rakesh told anyone at home about this bunk, he would be a dead man. These were the kind of things troubling his mind.

He completed his daily morning routine and put on his school uniform, It was 7AM by his watch. He was on his usual schedule. He tried to move out of his house as soon as possible, perhaps because he didn't wanted to face his father, to avoid a long and tedious lecture on character, good life, concentration, or focus.

Concentration and focus were his father's favourite topics to lecture him on. He took out his cell phone and called Dev, but his number was busy.

Shiv came out of his house and found Rakesh cleaning his car.

"Let's go, bhaiya?"

"Yes, let's go, Rakesh."

Rakesh started the car and Shiv sat next to him.

"We have to pick Dev up too."

"Okay, bhaiya ji. By the way, his bike will take the entire day to get fixed and will be ready by evening today. Where does he live?"

"He lives near Munshi Pulia Chowraha. You drive on, I will tell him to come to the main road."

"Okay, bhaiya ji."

Shiv took out his cell, dialled up Dev and said, "Hey Dev, I will be on the main road in front of your house in 5 minutes."

"Okay, dude. I will see you there."

In a few minutes, they were in front of Dev's house. He stepped out of his car and went over to Dev's house. He called Dev again.

"Hey buddy, I am standing at your main gate, but I have a problem."

"What problem?"

"I have my driver with me. How will I handle him?"

"What is the problem with him?"

"If he tells anyone about my first bunk in Lucknow, I will be dead."

"Hahaha. Is that what is troubling you?"

"It's not a joke, man. And yes, of course it is troubling me."

"Dude, you should have a setting with your driver or anyone for that matter, from whom you might have some work. Wait, let me come. I will handle it."

Dev cut the call and stepped out of his house the next moment.

"Come on, Shiv. You should not worry about such small issues."

The first thought that came to Shiv's mind was, Was it a small issue? Dev went to the driver's seat and said, "Hello Rakesh, how are you this morning?"

"I am great, bhaiya ji. How are you?"

"I am also good. Do you mind if I drive today?"

Rakesh looked at Shiv. Shiv nodded at him.

"No, no not at all, bhaiya ji." Rakesh opened the door, left the driver seat for Dev and went to sit in the back seat. Dev and Shiv sat in the front.

Dev exclaimed, "Now, it's time to rock and roll." We took off. Vrooommm...

This guy had balls, Shiv thought. In less than a minute, they were at the Polytechnic Chowraha.

"Wow, man. Don't you think you drive quite fast?" Shiv said, seeing that the speedometer was not going below 80 kmph. "Don't worry at all, man. I have been driving since 8th standard." It was quite obvious by the way he drove.

A few more minutes passed and they reached the Lohia Chowraha.

Dev stopped the vehicle near a pan shop, gave Rakesh a 500 rupee note and said, "Rakesh, please bring me a pack of Classic Milds, 10 Rajnigandha, and buy yourself whatever you need."

"Okay, bhaiya ji"

Dev took out his cell and dialled Khan.

"Where are you, buddy?"

"Where are you, man?"

"I am waiting for you at Lohia Chowraha"

"I will be there in 10 minutes."

"Okay."

"Khan is on his way," Dev told Shiv, who was wondering where the rest of the guys were.

"Bhaiya ji, your stuff."

"Oh, thanks Rakesh."

Dev took a cigarette, lit it up and blew smoke around his face. He looked at Rakesh.

"So Rakesh, have you been to Deva Shareef?"

"Yes, Bhaiya ji. I have been there. It's a very sacred place for the Muslims. They have a lot of faith in that place."

"Yes, that's true. That is why we have planned to go there today. You know, we had planned it a long time ago that we would go to Deva Sharif after the exams if we passed with good marks. With God's grace, we all passed with good marks indeed, so we have to keep our promise."

"So, you all will not be going to school today?"

"And you are not going to discuss this at all with anyone at home. Okay, Rakesh?" interrupted Shiv, making himself clear.

"Arrey, not at all, Bhaiya ji. I do not want to miss this opportunity to visit the holy place either. Bhaiya ji, do not worry at all."

"Here comes Khan."

Khan arrived on his black Pulsar 220cc.

"Hey Dev, how are you, man? And what are you doing with this new boy?"

"Hey, Khan. Ah well, his name is Shiv and my bike broke down yesterday, so this guy dropped me home. I invited him to come along with us to Deva Sharif."

"Okay, no problem then."

Khan turned to Shiv, gave him a friendly look and said, "Hi, I am Mustafa Khan. CALL ME KHAN."

"Hi Khan, I am Shiv. You call me Shiv only. So, where now?"

Dev: "I just talked to Chikna. He and Binnu are waiting at the Patrakarpuram Chowraha. We will have to pick them up from there. Khan, you can park your bike there too."

Khan: "If you were going to meet them there anyway, why the hell did you call me here, buddy?" He started giggling.

Dev: "As if I knew before that they are waiting there. Listen, cut the crap. Let's go."

Khan started his bike and zoomed off.

Dev: "Come on, Shiv, let's move. Get in, Rakesh."

Dev started their car and led it towards the Patrakarpuram Chowraha. It took them a few minutes to reach Patrakarpuram chowraha. Both were waiting for them there.

"Come on, guys. Get in," Dev said to everyone.

"Rakesh, you go to the back seat," Shiv told Rakesh.

Chikna: "Hey, Dev. Who's car is this?"

Dev: "Well, it's Shiv's."

Binnu: "Okay. Hey, Shiv."

Shiv: "Hey, Binnu."

Chikna: "Hi, Shiv. I am Mohit."

Shiv: "Hi, Mohit. By the way, I have heard everyone's introduction in the class."

Binnu: "Then it's okay, buddy."

Dev: "Oh, sorry guys, I forgot. Maya is waiting for us at the Divine Heart Chowk."

Shiv: "Let's move then, buddy. It's 9:45 already. Let's move fast."

Dev: "Oh yeah, babe."

The Scorpio started ruling the road as the D-company inside it headed towards Deva Shareef. Dev took out his cell and called Maya. "Hey, Maya. I am reaching your place in 10 minutes. I will wait for you at the main gate of the Divine Heart Hospital."

Shiv was quite happy to hear that a girl was coming with them as well. He felt a little nervous too as he has been in a boys' boarding school in Nainital all his life. He was shy and wasn't used to talking to girls at all.

Dev stopped the car at Divine Heart. "Come on, Maya. Get in quickly. We are getting late, yaar." As soon as Maya got in, they were back on their way to Deva Shareef.

Shiv was shocked to see Maya. HE was a healthy guy, dark in complexion, and with short hair. He was wearing their school uniform too. He had a very cute face cut, but his mouth was full of tobacco.

Maya: "Hello, guys! Wassupp!? Hey, Khan! When did you buy this new Scorpio, man?"

Khan: "It's not mine, buddy. Meet Shiv, by the way."

Maya: "Hi, Shiv. Nice meeting you, buddy."

Shiv: "Hey, Maya. The pleasure is all mine. I had been hearing about Maya so much that I thought that it would be some girl named Maya. I am totally shocked to see you instead. Is Maya your real name?"

Binnu: "Hahaha, you thought he was a gal? Hahahaha."

Chikna: "Shiv, his name is Mayank Verma. We used to call him Mayank, but then the movie 'SHOOTOUT AT LOKHANDWALA' came out and since then, Mayank has become Maya Bhai, the character that Vivek Oberoi played in the film."

Shiv: "Okay, so that's the story behind Maya."

Maya: "If the misunderstanding around my name has been sorted out, can we please badnaam Munni, Dev? Play the track, man. It's so awesome, yaar."

Dev: "Yeah, yeah, of course, why not? Shiv, play the track, buddy."

Amidst the music and the fun and games inside the car, Dev crossed 100, then 110, then 140 kmph. Binnu was busy creating smoke rings with his cigarette, and succeeded about 1-2 times in 10-20 tries. Shiv, on the other hand, found himself day dreaming about what must be happening back at school.

Prateek must be trying hard to solve some sum in maths class, Shiv thought. Mudit must be busy with the ladies of the class, and the Red House Prefect must be busy with her gang. Did I forget to mention her?

Well, there was this gal, name unknown, tall and fair with attractive brown eyes, shielded under specs. She had long silky hair and our buddy, Shiv, found her quite attractive. She continues to remain a mystery to him, however.

Shiv was lost deep in his thoughts, when Dev shook him and informed him that they had reached Deva Shareef. There was a big busy market around the dargaah. It was Shiv's first time visiting a dargaah.

Everyone took out handkerchiefs from their pockets to put on their heads. Shiv didn't have one, so he bought a new one from the market. The place had a sacred vibe to it.

• • •

It was blissfully quiet there and everyone was praying with sincerity and discipline. Only this group of boys were making a little bit of noise.

Dev: “Shiv, it is believed that all one’s wishes get fulfilled here. Ask whatever you want with a pure heart here.”

Shiv: “Okay, bro.”

They all had their darshan and came out of the dargaah. Everyone cleared their respective bills for the sacred offerings. Within a few minutes, they were on their way back to Lucknow.

Dev: “So guys, what next? Khan?”

Khan: “What next? I didn’t get it, bro. What devilish idea do you have in your mind, Pandit ji?”

Binnu: “Bhai, an hour and a half is still left before the classes get over at school. We can go for a movie.”

Dev: “No, idiot. You need two hours for a movie anyway. What about a chilled beer, guys? Anyone, any problem?”

Maya: “Bhai, you just stole the words from my mouth.”

Dev: “I understand your feelings, buddy. I receive them via Bluetooth, haha.”

Chikna: “Bluetooth? lols. Where will we get them?”

Dev: “Chill, yaar. There is a beer shop on the highway. All will have Kingfisher Strong, na? Rakesh babu, what will you have? Shiv, what will you have?”

All: “Aye aye, captain!”

Rakesh: “Yes, Bhaiya. I will have what you all will have, bhaiya ji.”

Shiv: “Bhai, I don’t drink.”

Dev: “Then start today. Today will be the auspicious day when you started having beer. All of us started just this summer too. We are also freshers here, buddy.”

Shiv: “Okay then, if you insist.”

Khan: “Hey, Dev. There’s the shop, bro. 1, 2, 3, 4, 5, 6, 7. Seven cans in all.”

Chikna: “Chakhna also, bhai. Bring Lays.”

Khan: “Come Maya, let’s go.”

Maya and Khan went out to get the beers. They were soon back with the beers, some chakhna and cigarettes.

A can of beer each was handed over to everyone. Dev was driving and Shiv was feeling hesitant to take his life’s first sip of beer. Dev noticed this hesitation.

He shouted, “Come on, guys. Today. our new friend Shiv is going to take the first beer of his life. Wish him good luck so that he keeps drinking life long without damaging his liver or Kidney so that he can remember us everytime he drinks beer. CHEERS GUYS!”

All: “CHEERS, BHAI!”

Everyone started to drink, but Shiv was still hesitant. Seeing this, Maya pushed his beer can upto his mouth. Shiv: “Yuck, it’s horrible, yaar. How do you guys drink it?”

Dev: “Hahaha, it feels like that the first time. You’ll find it bitter now, but after 2-3 sips, you will start liking it.”

Maya: “Egg-jactly, Dev. Come on, sip up. Be a man!”

Everyone was enjoying the trip and was having a good time when Shiv suddenly remembered his prefect girl again.

“Hey, Dev?”

“Yeah, dude!”

"Bhai, do you know this girl, the girl who is the Prefect for Red House. She wears glasses, is fair and has long hair."

"Well, I usually don't like those prefects, nor do they quite like me. They are the protectors of rules and I believe that rules are made to be broken, haha. They are not my friends, but I can find out who this girls is. Show her to me tomorrow."

"Thanks, bro."

"Anytime, bud."

"We all had such a great time today. You know what? I am starting to get really attracted to this girl. Why don't you find out everything about her?"

"I will, don't worry."

"You know, there is one more thing, bro."

"What?"

"I think I am high."

"Hahaha…I am high too, but only a little bit."

"Hahaha, you better concentrate on driving."

"Don't worry, man. I will drive you all safely to your houses."

Maya started singing the song 'Yeh dosti hum nahi todenge' from the rear of the car and everyone else joined him. This singing session went on for the entire way back. In less than 25 minutes, they were back at the Polytechnic Chowraha.

Dev: "Hey Khan, where did you park your bike?"

Khan: "Bro, it's at Sahara Plaza."

Dev: "I will drop you guys at Sahara plaza then."

They dropped Khan, Chikna and Maya at Sahara plaza. Dev: "Okay then, see you guys tomorrow. Bye."

Shiv: "Bye, guys."

Khan: "Bye, guys."

Everyone left for their respective homes.

Dev: "Binnu, I will drop you at Polytechnic chowraha. Is that okay, bud?"

Binnu: "Yeah, no problem."

In a few minutes, they dropped Binnu there and made their way back to Dev's house.

Shiv: "Okay then, Dev. See you tomorrow."

Dev: "Okay then, see you tomorrow. Will you please come aside for a minute?"

Shiv: "Yeah, sure."

Dev took Shiv away from Rakesh and said, "Keep in mind one more thing, Shiv. First, if Rakesh tells anyone about your bunk, you can definitely disclose his drinking habit to them. You are now safe. Secondly, now that you have Rakesh on your side, keep giving him money for beer on weekends, but don't start drinking with him."

"How are you able to think so much, man? And why should I not drink with him?"

"Because if you drink with him, what will you do with us, bro? Hahaha."

"Thanks for the tip, man. Shall I pick you up tomorrow?"

"No, I will see you directly at school tomorrow."

"Okay."

"Bye."

"Bye."

• • •

CHAPTER THREE

More than a month passed and life was going cool for Shiv, except that even after coming to school regularly for more than a week, Shiv was unable to find his prefect girl. It seemed as if she had just disappeared from school.

He hadn't seen her since that Deva Shareef trip.

One day, the assembly was taking a long time and it finished half an hour late than regular time. Shiv, Dev, Khan and whole gang was sitting in class, waiting for the rest of the students to join back.

Shiv was standing near the window from which the staircase was visible.

He exclaimed, "Hey, Dev! Come here, man. Quick, look there, yaar! There she is, the prefect girl."

Dev: "Who? Where?"

Shiv: "There, man. The tall girl with specs."

Dev: "Oh, that girl!"

Dev: "Hey, Maya. Come here, man."

Maya: "Yup?"

Dev: "You see that tall girl with specs there? Isn't she your girlfriend Aradhana's friend?"

Maya: “Oh, that girl? Yeah. Her name is Ishani Sharma and she’s in the Commerce section. Why are you enquiring so much, buddy?”

Dev: “Arrey chill, Maya. It’s not me, bro, it is Shiv.”

Maya: “Oh, is that so, Shiv?”

Shiv: “Come on, guys. Stop teasing.”

Maya: “So, what’s the scene, bro?”

Shiv: “Scene? Come on! I don’t even know her, yaar.”

Maya: “Oho. If you want to go for a movie with her, be there at Wave this Saturday. I will inform you about the movie.”

Dev: “Hahaha, Maya, you are so clever, man.”

Maya: “Arrey, I am already going for a movie with Aradhana. I will just ask Ishani to come along too and you both can meet us at Wave. What say, guys? Done?”

Shiv: “Done, buddy! 100%”

Dev: “Done, but that’s about Saturday. What about today?”

Maya: “Today? Let’s go and play pool after lunch break.”

Shiv: “How will we go out of the school before the last bell?”

Dev: “Lol, we will jump over the boundary, how else?”

Shiv: “Jump over the boundary? Are you crazy, man? It’s more than six feet high.”

Shiv couldn’t believe that these guys were jumping fences too.

It was lunch time and they all waited at the canteen till everyone had gone back to their classes.

Khan: “Come on. Let’s move, guys.”

Dev: "Yeah."

Khan and Dev led, while Shiv and Maya followed behind. They headed towards the primary wing, which only had till class V.

Khan: "Hey, Dev, the guard who's standing at the gate of the primary section is one of our men. He will let us pass."

Shiv: "Are you sure he will let us pass?"

Khan: "Just watch it, bro. Come with me, guys."

Khan started leading. Behind him went Dev, then Maya and then Shiv at the end. Khan told everyone else to stay about 3 meters behind him and to come forward only when he gave the signal.

Khan went to the guard and it seemed as if he was some kind of a devotee to Khan. Khan told him that they will be leaving and then signalled everyone to follow him out.

Everyone quickly started moving out of the gate. Khan was the last one to leave the premise. Before leaving, he put a 100 rupees note in the guard's upper pocket. He then rushed away from there.

In the meantime, Shiv and Dev went to fetch Dev's and Khan's bike. Maya sat behind Shiv and Khan took a seat behind Dev.

They rode away from the school, towards the Lohia Chowraha. Everyone stopped a few kilometres ahead, near a pan shop for cigarettes and masala.

Maya: "Bhai, let's go to MD."

Dev: "MD, at this time?"

Maya: "Yes, at this time. There will be no one there, we will sit in peace."

Khan: "Come on, let's go."

They started the bikes again and headed towards MD, but the one question that Shiv was struggling with was, 'What is MD?' He couldn't resist anymore and asked Maya who was trying to light a cigarette while sitting behind him.

"Hey, Maya. What is MD?"

"MD stands for Marine Drive."

"Marine Drive? But that's in Mumbai, na?"

"Mumbai? I don't know about Mumbai, but there is definitely one in Lucknow."

"Okay, but why are we going there? What will we do there? Are we going to eat bhel puri there?"

"Listen, dude. You are taking it wrong. Let me explain it to you. It's an empty road along the river Gomti. It is about 2-3 kilometers long and pretty wide. There is a DEAD END at one end of it. Since it is always empty and there is no traffic, The BIG BOYS of Lucknow use the road to race their bikes and cars."

"Ohoho! Is that so? It must be a fun place then."

"You are going to love it, buddy!"

Dev was speeding swiftly towards his destination, and Shiv followed him. In the company of Dev, Shiv had now started to drive quite fast too.

It took them just a few more minutes to reach MD. It was an open road with hardly any vehicles on it, yet wide enough for two cars to cross together at the same time. On one side of the road was Gomti, separated only by a long hedge of bushes There was also a footpath right next to it, that extended all the way to the dead end.

It was day time, yet there were about 4-5 riders on MD. According to Maya, most of the regular crowd came there during the evening time.

• • •

But on weekends, he told him, it looked no different from a film set, as they show in the 'Fast and Furious' movies, the places where the guns and the goons of the city race with their big machines.

Dev stopped right before the Dead End. Beyond the Dead End, there was a railway crossing a few kilometres ahead, separated only by a dusty trail.

Shiv: "So, this is MD?"

Khan: "Yes, Boss."

Maya: "Dev, I dropped my lighter, man. Do you have a lighter or a matchbox for lighting a cig?"

Dev: "Yeah, sure."

Dev took out a lighter from his pocket which looked very unique. It was the same lighter that SRK used in his film DON2. Yes, it was exactly the same.

Maya: "Hey! Dev, nice lighter. How much did you buy this one for, man? I want one too."

Khan: "Maya, it's a ZIPPO, baba. It is very costly."

Maya: "Hey Dev, please tell me how much did it cost."

Dev: "My brother gave it to me. On the box, it was printed Rs. 6999."

Maya: "I will also buy one, yaar. I will just have to jugaad 7000 bucks for it."

Dev: "Hahaha, exactly. JUGAAD!"

Khan: "Hey guys, it feels very boring here, yaar. Let's go my house, we'll play PSP."

Dev: "I thought we came out from school to play pool."

Khan: "Bro, I don't feel like going there. Come on, let's go home, yaar. It's nearer from here."

Shiv: "Come on, let's go to his place."

Dev: "Okay dokay, Captain!"

Again, the two bikes started with a roar zoomed away, creating a storm of dust behind. This time, the bikes did not stop anywhere before Khan's house.

It was a big house painted a gleaming white, with two Safaris and three or four gunmen standing outside the huge black front gates before his house. Everyone entered inside and sat in the drawing room.

A maid came in with Rooh Afja for everyone. Then came Khan's mom. She was a short statured, but very elegant lady. As soon as she entered the room, everyone stood up and went forward. First Dev, then Maya and then Shiv touched her feet for her blessings.

"Oh look, how much you all get tired after school! They teach too much at schools these days. Ramu, get dry fruits for everyone."

Dev: "Aunty please, we cannot take too much."

Khan's mom: "These are your growing years, beta. Have them. And who's this boy? I have never seen him before,"

Khan: "Mummy, this is Shiv. He is new to the school."

Khan's mom: "Okay. Feel comfortable, I have to go to the doctor."

Everyone: "Namaste, Aunty."

Khan's mom: "Namaste, beta."

Khan's mom left the room.

Shiv: "Aunty is going to the Doctor? What happened, Khan?"

Khan: "Yeah, she is suffering from some problem. I don't know. She hasn't told me."

Shiv: “Okay.”

Khan: “Guys, let’s go to my room.”

Everyone: “Yeah, let’s go.”

They all started for Khan’s room, when suddenly, Shiv’s eyes fell on the wall clock in the drawing room. It showed 14:00 hours. It had already been fifteen minutes since the school got over. Rakesh would be waiting for him outside the school, he thought.

Shiv: “Guys, I think it’s time to leave. The school got over at 13:45. Dev, can you please drop me back to school.”

Dev: “Sure, man.”
Khan: “Are you going back right away? We arrived here just now, yaar. Time passes so quickly once we are out of the class, man.”

Dev: “Yeah, bro. You are right.”

Khan: “Chalo then, I will see you tomorrow at school.”

Dev and Shiv came out. Dev started the bike and the three of them made their way back to the school where Shiv’s driver Rakesh was waiting for him to take him home.

Mayank has to be dropped at his house too. Dev dropped Shiv at school, then went away with Mayank.

On his way back home, Shiv started thinking about Khan’s mom and how much she trusted him. Even when they all had bunked half the classes, she welcomed them as if they had spent the whole day studying hard and were really tired after it. Yet, it was not true at all.

But this is what is called MAA KA PYAAR. A mother trusts her child a lot, she trusts blindly, no matter what the situation may be. Every mother trusts her child a lot.

Apart from this, Shiv knew that he was not studying at all. He had no idea how he would score good marks. He could imagine big zeros granted on his answer sheets. Deep in his thoughts, he didn't even realise when he arrived home.

• • •

CHAPTER FOUR

It was Saturday and it being the second one of the month, it was a holiday. Shiv, Dev and Maya had already planned to go for a movie. Shiv called Dev, "Hey dude, Ssup! What time is the movie?"

"Which movie?"

"Dude, you forgot about the MOVIE. The one that Maya and we are going for today."

"Oh, that. I thought it was a joke, man. I don't have any idea regarding that. I haven't even talked to Maya about it. Just give him a call and ask yourself."

"You don't seem quite interested in going there."

"Yeah, dude. I am not in a mood either. I don't go for movies usually, I find them quite boring."

"Oh, come on, bud. Let's go for a movie."

"Bro, it's of no use. I am not going for it, no matter what. Call Maya and enjoy yourselves."

"Are you sure you are not coming there with us?" "Dude, I know I am going to get bored there. I will catch up with you guys after the movie."

"Okay then, see you after that."

"Okay, have a nice time."

Shiv then dialled up Maya.

"Hey, Maya. Wassupp!"

"Nothing much, man. I was just about to call you. I was thinking we would go for 'THE AVENGERS'."

"That's cool. Where shall I meet you?"

"Dude, I have to pick Aradhana and Ishani from Aradhana's house, and you know these girls take a lot of time dressing up and with make up. I don't think I will be able to get there on time. You do one thing, you go to Wave, collect four tickets for the movie and then give me a call. I will pay you for the three tickets there."

"Okay, no problem, bro. Bye. See you there."

"Bye."

Shiv disconnected the call. He was finally going out with Ishani and he was quite excited. He went to take a quick shower. The movie was to start at 12:15 PM, thus he planned of leaving the house at 11:30. He took half an hour in the bathroom. First, he thought of wearing formal pants with a formal shirt, he had to impress the girl after all.

But then, he figured it would look way too mature if he wore that. He finally picked a torn jeans and paired it with a red Superman tee. After dressing up in that, he felt that he was looking too funky, and that it was better to wear a casual shirt in place of a tee. After 45 minutes, he was finally ready in a sky blue check shirt and dark blue rugged jeans, along with white shoes. Aha, now he looks perfect! Now it was time for him to get some money from his mother. (The only source of income for him.)

"Mom, mom, where are you?"

"I am in kitchen."

Shiv went to the kitchen.

• • •

"Oh! Where are you going? By the way, you look so smart."

"Mummy, I am going for a movie and I need some cash."

"Going for a movie? Great. How much do you need?"

"Mom, I actually have to buy tickets for 3 of my friends too, so can you give me a total of 2000 rupees? And I won't be coming home for lunch. We will have lunch there itself."

"With whom are you going?"

"Mayank and some girls from my class."

"Okay, first come here. *Teri nazar utaar dun.* You look so dashing today."

"Oh, mom!"

"*Aal tu jalal tu, aai bala ko taal tu; Aal tu jalal tu, aai bala ko taal tu…*" She repeated it 7 times.

"Okay, done now."

"Yes. Here, take your money and be back before your daddy comes home."

"Okay, bye mummy."

Rakesh was ready, waiting for him at the gate.

"Rakesh, let's go."

"Okay, Bhaiya ji."

"Come, sit next to me."

Shiv took the driver's seat again. He started the engine and zooooooom, he hit the road hard. In the company of Dev, he had become an expert driver.

As it was Saturday and a holiday, a lot of student crowd was there at the mall, either for the movie or for shopping. There was a long queue at the ticket counter of the cinema.

Shiv stepped out of the car and asked Rakesh to park it and then meet him at the ticket counter. As taught by Dev, he remembered that he had to take care of his driver too, so he bought five tickets from the counter. four for his group and one of Jannat 2 for Rakesh.

“Bhaiya ji, I have parked the car. Here are the keys.”

“And here is your ticket for Jannat 2.”

“Thank you, bhaiya ji. You always take such good care of me.”

“It’s okay. Just do one thing, I will call you when I get free. Till that time, you keep this 100 rupees and get your lunch at the dhaba on the backside of the mall. Okay?”

“Okay, bhaiya ji. Can you give me an idea of around what time you’ll call me?”

“I think, near about 4 PM.”

“Okay, bhaiya ji.”

“Okay, now go on and enjoy yourself.”

“Okay, bhaiya ji.”

Shiv was all by himself now. He took out his cell and called Maya.

“Hey, where are you, man?”

“I am at Aradhana’s place. Just leaving in 5 minutes.”

“Okay, I have bought the tickets, please come on time.”

“Will try my level best, buddy.”

“Okay.”

Shiv had nothing to do but to wait for the rest of them to arrive there. He decided to sit beside the Mr. McDonald’s statue outside the McD there, till they arrived.

• • •

It was 12:20 PM already, yet there was no sign of Maya. Shiv decided to call Maya again and just as he pulled out his cellphone, a grey Endeavour with a VIP number '1111' stopped at the gate and out came Maya, Aradhana and Ishani.

Mayank was wearing a smart red coloured check shirt, black jeans, a Gucci leather belt, black leather shoes and sexy brown aviators over his eyes. He was extremely well dressed, Shiv thought. Aradhana was an averagely tall girl with a fair complexion and long straight black hair. She looked gorgeous in the yellow top she was wearing along with light blue capris. As for Ishani...

Shiv was so lost in her eyes, that he didn't even notice how absolutely stunning Ishani looked in her white top and light blue jeans, sporting contact lenses in place of her regular spectacles.

Mayank signalled at his driver to go back and approached Shiv who had been sitting next to the Mr. McDonald's statue. Mayank and Aradhana looked gorgeous together. Surprisingly, they looked much older than their 11th standard selves.

Maya: "Hey, Shiv! Wassup dude? I hope we are on time."

Shiv: "Dude, you guys are just in time. I was about to give you a call."

Maya: "Meet Aradhana, my girlfriend."

Shiv: "Hey, how are you? I finally got the golden opportunity to meet you."

Aradhana: "Hey, Shiv. No dude, the pleasure is all mine. Thanks for collecting the tickets for us."

Shiv: "Oh, come on. You don't need to thank me at all. By the way, you look gorgeous."

Aradhana: "Really? Thanks."

Maya: "And this is Ishani, she is from the Commerce section."

Shiv: "Hey, Ishani."

Ishani: "Hi."

Shiv: "I have seen you at school. Aren't you the girl with the prefect badge, who is in charge of minding the students moving back to their classes after the morning assembly?"

Ishani: "Oh, yes. I am the same girl, but I monitor only in the absence of the Head Girl."

Maya: "Let's go for the movie, we are getting late."

Everyone: "Yeah, let's go."

After the movie

Maya: "I thought it was going to be an Iron Man show, but the Hulk rocked the last half an hour."

Aradhana and Shiv together: "Yeah, absolutely."

Aradhana: "It was an awesome movie, and the stunts were so amazing."

Shiv: "How did you find the movie, Ishani?"

Ishani: "Yeah, it was okay. I am not into these super hero movies actually, so I don't watch them much. The effects were amazing though."

Shiv: "Okay, so what kind of movies do you normally watch?"

Ishani: "Haha, well, I do not watch movies too often. I just watch them with friends. I do not watch any when I am alone."

Shiv: "Oh, I get it. You don't seem to be much of a movie freak."

Ishani: "Yeah, I'm not, but I read novels. Do you?"

Shiv thought, 'Who reads novels these days? She seems to be a book worm, that's why she has got such big glasses covering her beautiful eyes.'

Shiv: "Yeah, I do. I have read those Harry Potter books."

Ishani: "Harry Potter? Hahaha, I think that's for kids, not teenagers. Do you still read Harry Potter?"

Shiv tried to think of something intelligent to say, but was saved by Mayank's timely interruption.

Mayank: "Hey guys, I just received a call from my mom. I got to go. She needs me to go along with her to some uncle's place. Shiv, let's drop the girls, man."

Shiv: "Oh, let's go then, man. You shouldn't be late if your mom has called you. Let's go."

Aradhana: "Guys, I actually have to buy some stuff and Ishani too wants to buy herself a dress."

Shiv: "How will you guys go back then?"

Mayank: "Yeah, how will you guys go back?"

Ishani: "Don't worry, my mom will come pick us up or we'll take an auto. It's not an issue."

Shiv: "Are you guys sure? I can come back after I drop Mayank."

Aradhana: "Actually, we may take quite long. We will manage."

Mayank and Shiv: "Okay then, see you guys at school. Bye."

Aradhana and Ishani: "Bye, guys."

***

It was 7.30 AM in the morning. Shiv was standing outside Dev's house, waiting for him. Dev came out of his house, opened the door and entered the car. Rakesh was sitting in the back as usual.

Shiv: "Wassup, bro?!"

Dev: "Nothing much. You tell me, how was your movie?"

Shiv: "Oh, the movie was good."

Dev: "And things apart from the movie?"

Shiv: "Hahaha, you are an asshole. Yeah, that was also good. I talked to her, I mean, I am now formally introduced to her, all thanks to Maya bhai. I think she might be interested in me too."

Dev: "Oh dude, come on, don't jump to a conclusion. Understanding a girl's heart is harder than measuring the depth of an ocean."

Shiv: "Yeah, you are right. Let's not talk about this, change the topic. How was your weekend?"

Dev: "Oh, it was normal, nothing special. Dad had come home so I was not able to roam around much. As it is, our school life is so rocking, we are like celebrities here. What else can one dream of?"

Shiv: "We should remember then that every celebrity faces his/her tough times, and believe me dude, tough times are closing in. Half yearly exams are approaching. It is just a matter of a day or two before a notice regarding the exams gets posted on the notice board."

Dev: "Arrey, dude. It's just the half yearlies. What is there to worry about half yearlies, man?"

They had reached the school now. Khan and Mayank were waiting for them at the tea stall across the road from the school.

• • •

Shiv and Dev stopped there, Rakesh took the wheel and parked the car on one side.

Dev: "Hey guys, Ssup!"

Khan: "YO YO HONEY SINGHAAAAAA!!!"

Dev: "YO YO HONEY SINGHAAAAAA!!!"

Mayank: "Ssup, guys?"

Shiv: "What's this new YO YO thing, man?"

Mayank: "Khan was in Delhi for the weekend with his cousins. I think they made him listen to Honey Singh songs everyday. That's why he has been singing this ever since I met him."

Everyone laughed.

Shiv: "Let's get to school."

They all reached their class and found a notice already there on the notice board, announcing the dates of the half-yearly exams.

Mudit was talking to Chikna.

Mudit: "Man, we are now left with only a month before the half yearly exams."

Chikna: "Hmm, you must have covered the whole syllabus."

Mudit: "No dude, I have not even started studying yet. I was thinking of starting today, but I have come to know that we have our inter-school cricket tournament starting next week."

Chikna: "So you play cricket too?"

Mudit: "I am not a pro, but I do play averagely. Let's see if I get selected for the team. They have the trials today after the fourth period."

Chikna: "Today?"

Mudit: "Yeah, today. It's on the notice board."

Shiv was listening to their conversation closely. He then saw Prateek, his first friend in that school, and went to sit beside him.

Prateek: "Hey, dude. Ssup, man? Where have you been? You are not regular to school anymore. Are you okay? I hope you are well."

Shiv: "Yeah, dude. I am absolutely fine, just had been busy elsewhere. How are you? What is going on in the school?"

Prateek: "I am also good. Nothing much has been going on here. We have half yearlies approaching, but we are still left with so much syllabus to cover. The inter-school cricket tournament is starting in a week too. What was the sense in keeping a tournament right before the half yearlies. They should either postpone the exams, or the tournament."

Shiv: "Hmm, do you play cricket?"

Prateek: "No bro, it's a waste of time."

Shiv: "Then why are you worried about the tournament? You should be happy that you will get so much extra time to prepare, as you won't have to go and play the matches."

Prateek: "No dude, you don't get it. The students who are not playing have to go to the venue in the school bus and cheer for the school team. Attendance is compulsory for such events, so it will be a waste of time for me."

Shiv: "Oh, that's bad. Hey, by the way, since I did not attend school for so many days, can I get your notes on physics and chemistry and the other subjects that I have missed?"

Prateek: "Yeah sure, why not? But I have not brought those notebooks today, as we do not have any of those lectures today. I can bring them for you tomorrow. Will that be okay with you?"

Shiv: “Yeah dude, not an issue at all. Thanks, bro!”

Prateek: “The class teacher is coming. I suggest you get back to your seat.”

Shiv: “Okay, see ya later.”

Shiv went back to his seat next to Dev. The class teacher entered the class, took out her register and started taking attendance.

Khan: “Hey Mayank, I came to know that you went on a date with Aradhana and your mom called in between. Guys, just imagine Mayank losing his virginity and his mom’s call interrupts him. Hahahaha.”

Dev and Shiv started laughing.

Mayank: “You fatty, why don’t you imagine your mom calling while you are fucking those sluts of yours, hahahahaha.”

Shiv: “Stop it, you guys. Bhai, today is the cricket team selection for our school. I am going for the trials, is anyone of you coming?”

Dev: “Yeah, I was in the team last year also.”

Khan: “This year, I will also go for the selections.”

Mayank: “Yeah, sure they are going to take this motu in the team. He can’t even run a hundred metres.”

Khan: “Look who’s talking. People whose houses are made of glass should not throw stones to at others.” He sniggered.

Shiv: “Oh ho, they’ve started again.”

CHAPTER FIVE

The D-gang made their way to the ground for the cricket team trials. Many students had already assembled there. The Principal had debarred the class XII and X students from participating, as they had their board exams that year, so it was clear that the team would mostly comprise of students from class XI and IX.

Their sports teacher was a fat guy in his mid thirties. He had too much oil in his hair, dark skin, and a sumptuous Bhagat Singh/ Shikhar Dhawan style moustache. He wasn't too tall in height. With a pot belly hanging over his belt, he looked like a corrupt cop.

Dev: "Guruji, namaskaar!"

Khan: "Guruji, pranaam!"

Coach: "Namaskaar, namaskaar. How are you, boys? You guys don't come to the ground at all these days."

Dev: "Sir, we have been busy with studies."

Coach: "Had you guys been that busy with studies, you would have topped the school."

Khan: "Arrey sir, we have been busy, but in our own style."

Coach: "Leave that. I know Dev is genuinely here for the Cricket Team selection, but what are you doing here?"

Khan: "Sir, I have come for the selection too."

Coach: “Okay, then good luck to all of you boys.”

Shiv: “How do you play, man?”

Dev: “Averagely, not so good. I just know how to use a bat well.”

Coach: “As there are a lot of new faces here today, I want to ask if there are any students here who have played at school, district or state levels before.”

A few students raised their hands for having played at certain levels.

He then divided all the boys into two teams and made them play a friendly match against each other, which lasted till about 5 in the evening.

After the match, the Coach selected 10 people, which included all the district level players, and noted down their names in a list. He then asked them to come regularly for practice.

Unfortunately, no one from Shiv’s group made it to the final team.

Shiv: “Shit, man. Now I realise the effects of practice. Had I been playing regularly, I would had gotten selected in the team. I have not played for even a single day since 9th class.”

Khan: “Really man, had you been practising, then too you wouldn’t have been able to do anything. Accept your failure, bro.”

Shiv: “Arrey bhai, I really used to play, man.”

Khan: “So, what now, Dev?”

Dev: “I really need this certificate to show to my father.”

Khan: “Chalo then, let’s go talk to the Coach. I will become garam (hot tempered) and you become naram (cool tempered).”

Dev: “Let’s go.”

• • •

Shiv: "What is this 'naram-garam' you are talking about?"

Khan: "Just watch it, bud."

Dev, Khan and Shiv went to the Coach.

Dev: "Excuse me, sir."

Coach: "Yes, Dev?"

Dev: "Sir, we would also like to play in the school team."

Coach: "It is not possible now, the team has already been selected. You were a part of the trials yourself. What can I do now?"

Khan interrupted him and said, "If you cannot do anything, then who can, sir?"

Coach: "Mustafa, we have already selected the boys for the team. The tournament is in a week."

Khan: "Sir, who are the boys that have been selected?"

Coach: "Look, here is the list. We already have all the players for the team."

Khan took the list from him and counted the number of names written.

Khan: "Sir, there are only ten names here. Cricket is played with eleven permanent players and 5-6 extra players, no?"

Coach: "Arrey, one player we be finalised later."

Dev: "Arrey sir, when you had to finalise the team today, why have you left a place for a player empty? You won't take permission from Principal ma'am to use the ground for the trials again, would you? What is the matter, sir?"

Coach: "Dev beta, you are a smart guy. Don't tell anyone, but he is the son of Shiksha Adhikari, the Basic of Lucknow region. Vice Principal Ma'am has asked me herself to put him on the team. You know how it is, but he did not come to school today."

Khan (sarcastically): "Sir, this is not fair at all. We are struggling hard here to get into the team, and you are cheating us. Sir, I won't let this happen. Either you include us in the team or I will not let anyone from the school take part in the tournament."

Coach (angrily): "How dare you talk to me like that?"

Seeing the Coach getting angry, Dev interrupted, signalling at Khan to walk away. He turned to the coach and said, "Arrey sir, he is a fool. He don't know how to talk to teachers. He comes from a very affluent background, but he doesn't know how to respect his elders. Forgive him, sir."

Dev signalled at Khan to come back and apologise to the coach. Khan came back with an innocent face.

Khan: "Sir, I am so sorry, sir. I got angry. Sir, you only say, is it right to put someone on the team just because his father/mother is an influential person?"

Coach: "Arrey, what can I do in this matter?"

Dev (politely and in a low voice): " Sir, please keep us as extras, we just need the certificates to show at our homes. Nothing else, sir. Please, sir."

Coach: "Come in the morning tomorrow, I will see what I can do."

Khan, Dev and Shiv: "Thank you, sir."

All three of them came out of the school. Khan left for his home along with his driver, while Dev and Shiv took the way back to theirs.

Shiv: "I don't think he will keep us in the team."

Dev: "His father will also keep us in the team, dude. Just wait and watch. Everyone in the junior school used to know

Khan and me. Now that we have shifted to senior school and all the teachers are new here, that is the reason it's getting delayed. In junior school, each and every teacher there used to be our devotee. It is not a problem, we will make everyone a devotee here too."

Shiv: "And how are you going to do that, my dear friend?"

Dev: "You know, Shiv, the best thing about this world is that the people are greedy. If you need to get some work done by a materialistic person, you just need to fulfil their materialistic needs. I feel very happy that people do anything for money these days. I take it in a positive way, which means, you can get anything done in this materialistic world by simply giving them material benefits. So, don't worry."

Dev took out his cell phone and dialled Khan's number.

Dev: "Hey dude, ssup!"

Khan: "Just changing, you say?"

Dev: "Listen, you own a mango orchard at Kursi road, don't you?"

Khan: "Yeah, my brother looks after that. What happened?"

Dev: "Do one thing, send your brother with 5-10 kg mangoes and a packet of the best sweets from Madhurima/Neelkanth to the Coach's house."

Khan: "Okay, no problem. Don't worry, my brother is good with bribing people. He does that to every engineer from PWD to get contracts."

Dev: "Hahahaha. That's great. Okay then, see you tomorrow."

Shiv: "What will happen now?"

Dev: "Now, we will play for the team, man. what else? Watch it tomorrow."

• • •

Shiv: “Okay, here we are at your house. Be ready in the morning tomorrow. I will pick you up at 7 AM sharp. Bye.”

Dev: “Okay, bye. See you tomorrow.”

Dev alighted from the car and went inside his house.

Shiv looked at his watch. It was 7 PM now. He had gotten very late, but he had a valid excuse. Shiv was driving back to his home, when Rakesh said, “Bhaiya ji, memsahib called on my cell to enquire about you.”

“Hmm, what time did she call?”

“Bhaiya ji, at 3 PM. She told me to ask you to call her as soon as you got free.”

“And you are telling me this now? Call her from my phone.”

“Okay, bhaiya ji.”

Rakesh dialled memsahib’s number and gave it to him.

It took her three rings to pick up the call.

“Beta, where have you been? It’s evening already and you haven’t reached home yet.”

“Mom, we had trials for the cricket team at school today, so I got late. I just got free and am reaching home in just 5-10 minutes.”

“Cricket team? Okay, okay. Come home soon, Choudhary uncle is waiting for you here.”

“Choudhary uncle?”

Before Shiv could ask any further, she cut the call. Now who was this Choudhary uncle, was the only question in his mind.

As he had spent most of his life at boarding school, he was not familiar with the uncles or aunties who frequently visited his family. He thought that perhaps Rakesh would know something and decided to ask him.

"Rakesh, do you know any Choudhary ji?"

"Who, bhaiya ji? R. P. Choudhary?"

"Who is this R. P. Choudhary?"

"He is a friend of bade saab. He is also from the same party as bade saab. After last year's elections, he become the minister of state for law and order. He also has many businesses. His transport business comprises of more than 150 trucks, I have heard. He also has a flour mill, a rice mill and many other such businesses. He and bade saab have been friends for a very long time. Both of them had entered politics together. He is the number three man in the state government, after CM sahib and deputy CM sahib."

"Oh, he sounds like a big shot. But why the bloody hell is he waiting for me?"

"We will come to know as soon as we reach home."

"Yeah, you are right, my friend."

***

As soon as Shiv reached home, he noticed a white ambassador car with a red beacon over it standing just outside his house. Next to it was a driver in white uniform and a gunman in black uniform. Apart from the white ambassador, there was also a white Honda City parked there with its own driver in a white uniform.

Shiv didn't make eye contact with anyone, but just walked straight inside. When he entered the drawing room, he saw a man sitting on the left sofa, along with his young son who seemed to be the same age as Shiv.

On the right sofa was sitting a woman along with a young girl.

Shiv's mom: "There you are! What took you so long at school today?"

Shiv: "Yeah, mom. That team selection took quite long."

Shiv's mom: "Here, meet Choudhary uncle."

Choudhary uncle was the man sitting on the sofa. He was tall and healthy with shiny black hair.

Shiv bowed down in front of him to take his blessings.

Shiv: "Namaste, uncle."

Choudhary uncle: "God bless you, son."

Shiv mom: "And this is Luv."

Shiv: "Hello, Luv."

Luv: "Namaste, bhaiya."

Shiv: "Namaste, bhai."

Shiv: "This is Mrs. Verma. She is the editor of The Times of Lucknow, the leading newspaper of the city."

Mrs. Verma was a gorgeous woman who looked great in the red saree she was wearing. Shiv bowed down in front of her too to take her blessings.

Shiv: "Namaste, aunty."

Verma Aunty: "Hello, beta. This is my daughter, Priyanka."

Shiv: "Hey, Priyanka."

Priyanka: "Hi, Shiv."

Shiv's mom: "Luv and Priyanka have also joined your school recently."

Shiv: "Oh, that's great. Which section are you in, guys?"

Priyanka: "I am in the commerce section, G."

Shiv: "Yeah, that is the commerce section. What about you, Luv?"

After thinking for a little bit, he said, "They have not given me a section yet."

Shiv: "Okay. Guys, if you'll all just excuse me for a bit, I'll quickly take a shower and be right back."

Priyanka: "Yeah, sure."

Shiv stood up and went to his room. He grabbed a towel and went to the bathroom to take a shower.

There was just one thing going on in his mind, that he had to be careful around Luv and Priyanka, as they both had now become his family friends. If he got involved in any mischief at school, they both might come to know about it and tell their parents. Ultimately, it could become a cause of embarrassment for him and his family.

He noticed that Luv was trying over and over again to avoid joining any conversation. He was either very shy and introverted, or he was hiding something.

'But what would he hide from a stranger like me?' Shiv thought. His mind full of various such thoughts, he took his shower. He then went to his room to change.

Shiv had just applied his Gatsby Deo and had pulled on a shirt, when someone knocked at the door.

"Yeah, who's there?"

"Hey, this is Luv. Can I come in?"

"Just a second, dude."

Shiv hastily pulled on a jeans and went to the door to open it.

"Shiv bhai, I am sorry to disturb you, but I was getting so bored there, so aunty told me to come to your room."

"Arrey, don't fret. You are always welcome, bro. Have a seat."

"Thanks."

"And Priyanka? Is she still out there with everyone else?"

"No, she is in your sister's room."

"Okay."

Now that no one was there except the two of them, Luv was feeling comfortable. Shiv closely observed his demeanour. He was quite tall, about 5 feet and 10/11 inches.

He was not as tall as his father, though. His face was square shaped. He had straight hair that were perfectly combed. He had a muscular built. He was wearing bellbottom trousers!Shiv couldn't believe what he was seeing. This guy was wearing bellbottoms, similar to the ones that Amitabh Bachchan used to wear in his late 70s hits.

His shirt was white and well ironed, the colour preferred by all politicians in the country. This revealed that he had a similar interest in politics as his father.

Luv did not seem like the only son of such a rich and powerful politician, though. Shiv started the conversation "So how much percentage did you scored in Tenth?"

"Hmm, I scored 58 percent marks, and you?"

"Leave that, bro. So, are you interested in Commerce or Science?"

"I do not have a problem with either. I can manage with any stream. Which stream are you in, bro?"

"I am in Science stream."

"Okay, which section?"

"It's D."

"Okay. I have heard about the school a lot. It is the most reputed school in Lucknow, and I have also heard that the students in this school are very hi-fi. Is that true?"

"No, bro. It's just a normal school. Yeah, there are some hi-fi elements, but it's not an issue."

"Actually, i have always been a very shy and introverted kind of a person. I do not interact with people much. That's why I do not have a lot of friends either."

"Arrey, don't worry about that at all. I am there for you. Do not worry at all, bro. Just hope that you get into my section too."

"Don't worry about that, bro. I will tell papa to get me in your D section, that will not be a problem. He will take care of it. I was just a little nervous about the new place, as i didn't know anyone there. But now, I am okay, bro."

"That's great, bro. Don't worry, you will be great."

"Thank you, bro."

"Any time, bro. Hey, by the way, do you always wear these bell-bottoms?"

"Yeah, all my trousers are like this. Does it look bad?"

"No, dude. It looks great. Whenever you go shopping next, just take me with you. I will help you with your clothes."

Shiv thought that Luv did not understand anything, but Luv was just shy, he was not a fool. He definitely got the hint that something was wrong with his dressing style. However, he did not said anything at that time.

Meanwhile, Shiv's mom entered the room.

"Luv, your father is calling you. He just got a call from the ministry. He has some urgent work for which he has to leave."

Luv: "Okay then, Shiv. Give me your contact number, I will see you at school."

Shiv and Luv exchanged contact numbers and bid adieu to each other. Shiv came out to see them off. Mrs. Verma and Priyanka were also standing at the main gate along with Choudhary uncle. Both of their drivers opened the car gates for their owners.

"Okay then, bhai sahab, I will take your leave now. I am getting late," said Chaudhary saab.

"Of course," said Shiv's dad humbly.

"Okay then, Shiv, see you at school," Luv said to Shiv.

"Sure, buddy. Goodnight."

"Bye, Luv. Bye, Shiv," said Priyanka and got into her car along with her mother.

"Bye, Priyanka," said a confused Luv and sat in his car.

Shiv: "Bye, Priyanka."

They all left. Shiv and his family went inside. Dinner was served for everyone.

Shiv retired early after dinner as he had to wake up early the next morning to go to school. He changed into his night suit and went to bed.

Shiv continued to think about Luv. He now had a shy guy for a new friend, who seemed to be very down to earth, perhaps because he was from a small town called Basti. What effect will Lucknow have on him, he thought. Only time had the answer to that question.

'What effect had Lucknow had on Shiv?' was the real question. He had stopped studying completely. He has started enjoying life, he had started having fun. What would happen in the exams, God only knew.

• • •

Suddenly, his phone pinged. It was Dev on WhatsApp.

"Hey, dude. What time will you come tomorrow, bro?"

"Hey bro, I will be there at your house by 6:30 AM. Ask Mayank and Khan to be there on time too."

"Okay, I will be ready."

"Have you talked to Khan regarding the Coach thing?"

"No, bro. Not yet."

"Are you sure that this will work?"

"It will, bro. Good night, see you tomorrow."

"It better work. Goodnight."

• • •

CHAPTER SIX

Shiv, Dev and Mayank were standing at the school ground, but there was no one there except for the few students who had been selected the previous day. Within just ten more minutes, almost all the selected students had reached the ground.

Mayank: "What happened, where is that sports teacher?"

Dev: "No idea. Look, there is the assistant sports teacher. Let's see what's happening."

Shiv: "Arrey baba, leave whatever is happening. Where is Khan? Did you call him?"

Mayank: "Mota must still be sleeping, what other work does he have?"

Dev: "He did not pick the call."

Mayank: "I already told you, mota must be sleeping, hahaha."

Suddenly, all the students went to fetch their bags and started moving to their respective classes.

Shiv: "What happened, yaar? Where is everyone going, and why?"

Dev: "Let me check."

Dev went ahead and stopped a boy to enquire what had happened.

Dev: “The key of the store room is with the Coach and he has not come yet. He will be coming after the morning assembly, so everyone has been asked to go to their respective classes.”

Mayank: “What do we do now?”

Dev: “Come, let’s go for a cigarette break.”

Shiv: “Let’s go.”

***

Everyone settled in class after the assembly. Kavita ma’am was there for the first lecture.

Mayank: “Did Khan call you back, Dev?”

Dev: “No bro, he hasn't yet.”

Shiv: “I don’t think he will be showing up today.”

Dev: “It seems like that.”

The sports prefect then entered the class with ma’am’s permission. He was a fair, tall, healthy and a very smart looking boy. He walked closer to the teacher’s desk and said something to her.

Her eyes widening as she shouted, “Silent, class! Can you not see that someone is here in the class.” This was followed by a pin-drop silence in the class. The sports prefect returned back after finishing his job.

Kavita ma’am: “Shiv and Dev?”

Shiv and Dev: “Yes, ma’am?”

Kavita ma'am: “I did not know that you guys play cricket, neither did anyone else in the class tell me that we have three boys from our class who are playing in the school cricket team. Where is Mustafa? He is in the team too.”

Everyone in class started shouting and howling. Dev and Shiv smiled at each other.

Kavita ma'am: “You both are required to go to the ground immediately. Your attendance will be marked for the day, so you need not worry about that. Now you may leave.”

Shiv and Dev: “Thank you, ma’am.”

Kavita ma'am: “Make us proud, boys.”

Shiv: “We will, ma’am.”

They walked out of the class and made their way towards the ground.

Shiv: “YES, YES! It seems like Khan’s strategy worked out.”

Dev: “I told you already, but where is that asshole?”

They reached the ground to find that Khan was already present there, sitting on the ground and absorbing vitamin D from the Sun. He was wearing his black RayBan glares, as if he had come to a garden.

Dev: “Mote, you are sitting here? I tired myself out calling you all morning. Where is your cell phone, man?”

Khan: “Arrey Dev bhai, I forgot my phone at home, yaar. When I reached school this morning, I was making my way upstairs to the class when the Coach met me on the stairs and pulled me back to the ground saying, ‘Come, beta. You are in the team, you have to practice,’ and I have been here since then, just practicing some throws.”

Shiv: “Hahaha. That’s all right. What happened yesterday?”

Khan: “Arrey, Shiv bhai, don’t ask what happened. Yesterday, when my brother went to The Coach’s house, he took a gunner with him too. On reaching his house, The Coach started saying, ‘Mustafa is like my own son, bhaisaab. You could have just given me a call, there was no need for you to come here.' Hahahaha..."

Dev: "I know how these teachers are. I told you, Shiv, it's going to work."

Shiv: "Yeah, man. I still can't believe, but it has happened."

Khan: "Don't worry, Shiv. If Allah wishes it, we will win the tournament too. Frankly speaking, I am happy just sitting here. Getting attendance of free is what I like the most."

Dev and Shiv laughed.

***

The tournament was to start on Friday and last for four days. There were a total of eight schools participating. A registration fee of Rs. 5000 was to be paid by each participating school.

Teams from all the schools were practising very hard to win the tournament. Khan was enjoying his position as an extra player. He came to school every morning and whenever he got tired, he used to pick up his bag and go back home. He was enjoying himself to the fullest.

Shiv, on the other hand, was practising very hard to get back in his form, along with Dev.

A team of girls from class 11th was also chosen to cheer on the team during the matches. This team of cheer leaders practiced their routine in the auditorium.

This cheering aspect was the gift of the one and only IPL, the Indian Paisa League. After the illegal bettings relating to it were exposed, it seemed as if nothing in this country could work without corruption or the involvement of money.

Shiv was getting back on track. He was promoted to be the first replacement. Dev and Khan didn't seem all that interested in the game.

All the classes were called off on Friday. The eight teams playing were,

Lucknow Montessori School

Lucknow Public College

La Martinier College

St. Francis Convent

St. Dominic College

Study Home

Sherwood School

Spring Academy

The matches were scheduled in the hierarchy of four quarter-final matches, two semi-finals between the winners of the last four matches, and then the Finals between the two final winning teams.

The matches were in T20 format, again thanks to IPL for having made it so popular.

All the matches were to be held at the City Stadium. Everyone was to report to school at 7 in the morning, from where, they were to be escorted to the stadium by the school buses.

The school team was taken to the stadium even earlier in another van. Khan had already told the the Coach that he, Shiv and Dev will join the team directly at the stadium.

Dev was driving the car. Shiv was sitting beside him. Khan, Mayank, Binnu and Chikna were sitting behind, while the driver, Rakesh, sat at the very back. Everyone had their cigarettes in their hands.

Dev: “Guys, what is the time?”

Chikna: “Bhai, it is only 7:15.”

Binnu: "Dude, the match will start at 8. We need to reach there on time."

Dev: "But it is not our match, is it? Ours is in the second shift. Right, Khan?"

Khan: "Yeah, bro."

Dev: "In case you are not so sure, you can always call your son and ask him."

Mayank: "Son? Mote, when did you get married? You didn't even invited us. Do you have a bastard now?"

Khan: "What nonsense are you talking, Dev?"

Dev: "I meant the the Coach, your new devotee. You have made him a proper bhakt of yours."

Khan: "Oh that, yeah, yeah. You know how I am."

Mayank: "The first match is between La Marts and Dominic. Both are all-boys schools. There won't be a good crowd in the audience. What will we do there?"

Shiv: "So, what do you have in mind? What do you want to do?"

Mayank: "I am just saying that we will get bored there. Nothing else."

Khan: "I think Mayank needs a beer, man."

Mayank: "Khan, you are my best buddy, man. You always know exactly what I want."

Chikna: "Dude, Mayank, it's not even 8:00 AM. Where on earth are you going to get beer right now?"

Mayank: "At what time can I get a beer then, man?"

Chikna: "How do I know, man?"

Dev: "Yeah, how would you know. We have always had beer either in the afternoon, or in the evening, or at a bar.

Actually, we have never thought about beer so early in the morning before."

Shiv: "Is there anyone here who knows at what time does the beer shop open?"

"It opens at 11:00 AM"

Everyone in the car turned to see who was this drunkard in the group who knew even the opening and closing times of a beer shop. To everyone's surprise, it was Rakesh, sitting at the back with an innocent expression.

Everyone started laughing seeing his innocent face.

"Does that mean we'll have to go to the match all dry?" asked a saddened Mayank.

"Don't worry, Mayank. Our match is in the second shift. I am sure we can get you beer by then," consoled Dev.

"Arrey, kaal kare so aaj kar, aaj kare so ab (what you have planned for tomorrow, do it today; what you need to do today, do it right away)," said a smiling Khan and started taking out beer cans from his school bag.

"HURRAY, HURRAY, HURRAY!" exclaimed everyone in the car.

Mayank: "Khan, Zindabad! Zindabad! Khan, you are my best brother. You always take care of me, bro. I will give you a Munna Bhai's jaadu ki jhappi"

Khan: "Just enjoy, bro, No need for a jhappi, hahahaha."

Everyone in the car had a can of Carlsberg in their hand, except for Shiv. Shiv resisted having beer, but when everyone was having such a high time, how could they have allowed him to go dry?

After Mayank blackmailed him by saying, "If you are my friend, you will take a sip," he had to surrender and take a sip.

• • •

PitBull's 'Hotel Room Service' was playing on the music system in the background. Everyone was having a great time. Suddenly, Binnu shouted, "Bhai, let's go to Marine Drive. Let's see what is happening there."

"Marine drive? Have a smoke, buddy, and by the time you finish it. we will be at MD," Dev said, turned the car towards Marine Drive.

***

Marine Drive was completely empty in the morning. Dev drove the vehicle all the way to the dead end, their favourite place. All the boys got down from the car and Binnu, Mayank and Khan sat down on the road and started calling everyone to join then for a snap.

To save memories in the form of snaps was a favourite hobby of Khan. He handed over his iPhone to Rakesh and told him to click a few pics of the group.

Suddenly, they heard roaring engine sounds coming from behind them. Everyone turned around in surprise to find three bikers approaching, one on a black Apache and two on Pulsars, a red 180cc and a black 220cc.

All three of them were approaching the place at a very high speed. They stopped at the dead end, about hundred metres before the place where Shiv and his friends were chilling.

The biker with the red bike was a very tall guy in a red shirt and dark blue jeans. The one on the black apache was an averagely tall guy wearing a light blue tee and sky blue jeans, while the one on the black 220 pulsar was again a tall guy wearing a yellow tee and black jeans.

They turned their bikes and stopped. The boys on the Apache and the Pulsar 220 sat on their bikes, while the one with the red Pulsar 180 stopped his bike in the middle of the road, waited there for a second, then raised his front wheel in the air the very next instant. The guy was now riding on the single rear wheel, that too without a helmet on his head.

Everyone from Shiv's group looked at them in awe, with their jaws hanging open. Chikna was the first one to say, "Hey guys, this is what they call a 'Wheelie', na?"

Binnu: "Yeah man, I remember seeing it in the movie Fast and Furious."

Khan: "Arrey, it was also in the movie Dhoom, na."

Mayank: "Yeah bro, I have noticed it too. How do these guys do this, man?"

Dev: "Arrey, it is not that difficult. I have seen my brother's friends do this too."

Shiv: "Are you sure, man?"

Dev: "Yeah bro, I have seen them do a wheelie, but they just do a 5-10 seconds' wheelie. I have never seen anyone riding on the rear wheel before. This is the first time."

Mayank: "But how do they do that, man?"

Dev: "My brother told me that you need to pull the accelerator in first gear for it and then leave the clutch suddenly. The front wheel will then jump off, after which, all you need to do is just balance."

Mayank: "It must be a difficult job na, bro?"

Shiv: "Oh, come on, bro. Tell me, which job is easy?"

Mayank: "Chilling at MD with beer in one's hand is definitely easy, man."

Khan: "Hahaha. Yeah, it is."

The bikers seemed to be well trained in what they were doing as they performed various stunts like wheelie, stoppie, rolling stoppie and Christ, to name a few.

• • •

Shiv had heard a lot about what MD looked like on the weekends, but he had not got a chance to go there on any weekend yet.

• • •

CHAPTER SEVEN

The sun was at its peak and it was 1:30 PM by Shiv's watch. After having lunch at Pizza Hut, the guys were on their way back to the stadium. Dev was driving.

Mayank had taken the back seat as he had had three cans of beer and a very heavy lunch. He was now sleeping calmly without troubling anyone.

Binnu and Chikna were having a smoke. Khan was feeling quite sleepy too. Dev was energetic as always.

Someone's phone started ringing. Oh yes, it was Khan's phone.

Shiv: "Khan, your phone is ringing, man."

Khan: "What?"

Shiv: "Binnu, check who's calling on his phone."

Binnu pulled out Khan's cell from his pocket.

Binnu: "It is from his home."

Dev: "Wake him up, Binnu bhai. Tell him it is a call from his home."

Binnu tried waking Khan up. After strongly nudging him twice, Khan finally woke.

Binnu: "Khan, it's a call from your home."

Dev: “Khan bhai, will you be able to talk? It is a call from your home.”

Khan: “Yeah, yeah, I am alright, bro.”

Dev: “Okay.”

The music in the car was turned down so that Khan could talk peacefully.

“Salaamwalekum, ammi.”

“Walekum.”

It took Khan a few seconds to realise that it wasn’t his mom, it was his father. He responded quickly, “Salaamwalekum, papa.”

“Walekum”

“Yes, papa?”

“Where are you right now?”

“Papa, I am at the stadium. We have a cricket match, I am playing for the school team.”

“Okay. Is it possible for you to come home right now? Can you manage? It is urgent.”

“No problem, papa. I will leave right away. What happened, papa?”

“Come home, then I will tell you.”

“Okay, papa.”

The call was disconnected. Without loosing a minute, Khan came to his senses.

Khan: “Guys, I’ll have to go home. It was papa, and he has called me home right away.”

Shiv: “What happened, bro?”

Khan: “I don’t know, yaar. He just ordered me to come back home as fast as possible.”

Shiv: “It will take only 2 minutes to reach the stadium from here, then Rakesh will drop you home. Will that be fine, bro?”

Khan: “Okay, make it quick.”

Dev: “Do not forget to take something for your mouth. Beer smells badly.”

Khan: “Yeah, I will take something on the way back.”

Shiv ordered Rakesh to drop Khan to his house. Mayank was fast asleep, almost passed out in his inebriation. Dev thought it wise to let him sleep in the car only. Everyone else made their way back to the ground.

The students of Lamarts and Dominic had left the ground, and only the team members and some cricket fans from those schools were waiting for the next match, which was to begin at 4 PM.

The next match was between Study Home and LMS. Since both these schools were co-ed, a gorgeous crowd had come from both sides to cheer for their teams.

LMS didn’t allow its girl students to wear skirts, and their uniform was salwar and kurta, whereas the girls from Study wore short skirts. So, all the guys were eyeballing them.

Only the school cheerleaders from LMS were allowed to wear skirts. They looked gorgeous.

The school teams had been allotted two green rooms to keep all their belongings and change. LMS team’s kit had a red tee and white track pants, while Study hall was in all-blue.

Shiv and Dev changed into their jerseys and came back to the ground. Winners of the previous match, the Lamarts team was now enjoying lunch.

The Coach had summoned everyone to the changing room at 3 PM to discuss the day's strategy. It was only 2:15 then. Shiv, Chikna, Binnu and Dev were sitting near the stands.

Dev's phone was ringing. It was Mayank on the other side.

"Hey, bro. Where are you?"

"Hey, Mayank. Are you awake now?"

"Yeah, dude. I have had my share of sleep. Khan woke me up before leaving."

"We are sitting near the stands. Come quickly," Dev said and disconnected the call.

Binnu: "Dude, Study Home girls are gorgeous, man."

Shiv: "Yeah, bro. You are right."

Chikna: "Bro, girls in our school are hot too. They just don't look very hot because of their traditional uniforms."

Binnu: "You mean, because of the salwar kurta?"

Chikna: "Yes, exactly. Look at those cheerleaders. They look so good."

Dev: "The school authority only chose pretty girls to be the cheerleaders."

Mayank: "If cheerleaders won't be pretty, how will the players feel motivated? Hahaha!"

Dev: "Yeah, Maya bhai. Welcome back, dude."

Chikna: "Look at that girl, guys. The girl in our cheerleading team…"

Mayank: "Which one, bro?"

Chikna: "That fair one in the centre, with long hair."

Mayank: "She's maal, yaar. Look at her sexy legs."

“Where, guys? Which one?” Dev, Shiv and Binnu asked all at once.

Mayank: “There, guys. Look at our cheerleading team. The girl right at the centre.”

There stood a hot looking, tall and fair girl, who was wearing a blue tee with a white skirt. These guys could only get a side glimpse of her.

Mayank: “Dude, I am going to get a better view.”

Chikna: “Buddy, I am coming with you.”

Shiv: “Guys, you won’t need to. Look, she’s turning this way herself.”

Mayank: “Bhai, she’s looking this way!”

Chikna: “Oh yes, she’s looking this way.”

Mayank: “Bhai, she is not only looking here, she is coming this way too. Do you think she heard my comment? I hope she is not a friend of Aradhana.”

The hot girl was approaching the group in just a few more seconds, she was there. Mayank tried to hide himself behind Dev, but the hot girl didn’t even noticed him. She went straight to Shiv.

“Hey, Shiv. Supp? Remember me?”

“Hey, I am good. How are you? Sorry, but I really can’t seem to remember you.”

“Ah well, then let me remind you. I am Priyanka Verma. I came to your house with my mom the other day.”

“Oh, yeah! I am so sorry, Priyanka. Please accept my apology. It was such a short meeting that day, so I was unable to recognise you today. I assure you, it will never happen again.”

“You are also on the team, it seems.”

"Yeah, and you are in the cheering team."

"Right you are."

"I hope your team's cheering helps us win this game."

"Oh, come on. It's not cheering team, but the playing team which will win the match."

"I hope so."

"I just saw you, so came here to wish you luck."

"That's exactly what I need the most at this particular moment."

"All the best, buddy. Make us proud."

"Thanks a lot, Priyanka."

"Okay then, see you later."

"Sure. Bye."

"Buh-bye."

Priyanka went back. Shiv turned around to find the rest of the guys staring at him.

Shiv: "What?"

Mayank: "You asshole! Why the bloody hell did you not tell us that you know that girl?"

Shiv: "Bro, I really didn't recognised her. She looks so hot today, but believe me, when I met her last, she was with her mom, that too in a salwar suit. How do you expect me to remember her?"

Chikna: "Cut the crap, guys. Let's not push it further. By the way, bhai, what is her name?"

Shiv: "Her name is Priyanka Verma."

Mayank: "Which class is she in?"

Shiv: "She is a new admission in the commerce section."

Binnu: "Bhai, please introduce me to her next time. Please, bro!"

Shiv: "Pakka, but next time."

Mayank and Chikna: "Bhai, we are also there to be introduced."

Shiv: "By the way, where is Dev?"

Dev had not been there with the group.

Mayank: "Yeah, man. Where is he?"

Mohit: "He was here just a while ago, man."

Binnu: "Look, he is there, bro!"

Everyone turned around to find Dev sitting under a tree, just beside the food stall where a group of students from Study Hall were having their food.

Shiv: "Oh yeah, he is there. I will be right back."

Mayank gave Shiv an angry look and said, "Bhai, promise me, you will introduce me to Priyanka."

"Yeah definitely, bro. I will introduce you to Aradhana," Shiv replied sarcastically.

Shiv went up to Dev. Dev was sitting there alone and brooding, which was strange for a social person like Dev. He always enjoyed being in his group. Shiv had never seen him alone anywhere.

"Hey, dude. Ssup? Why are you sitting here alone?"

Dev didn't reply. It seemed as if he was paying all his attention to what he was doing.

Shiv said again, "Hey, dude. What happened? You okay, bro?"

Without losing the focus of his eyes, Dev replied, "Bhai, she's looking so cute."

"Who's looking cute, bhai?"

"Bhai, that girl there, in that Study Hall group."

He pointed to a group of Study Hall students, comprising of 5 boys and 4 girls. All those students seemed to be in class 11th. There was this averagely tall girl there with straight hair and very fair skin, who was sporting black glares. She looked gorgeous.

In fact, all the girls in that group looked gorgeous and beautiful, but Dev couldn't look beyond that fair and cute girl.

Shiv expressed his thoughts, "Yeah, bro. She looks gorgeous. Go, talk to her."

"Talk to her? Are you crazy? I don't even know who she is."

"Dude, until and unless you talk to her, how will you come to know who she is?"

"Dude, you know I am too shy to talk to a stranger. I can't do it, bro. Think of something else."

"Okay then, we will find another way to get to know her."

"Dude, it's three. I think we should head back to the changing room. Remember, we have a strategy meeting."

"Oh yeah, we do. Let's go."

"Hey, dude. What about Khan? Will he come to play or not?"

"Let me check that. He might not be interested in playing, but he will definitely be interested in our gorgeous cheerleading team."

"Hahaha, you are definitely right."

• • •

***

Dev had been trying to reach Khan for the past ten minutes, but he was not picking up his phone.

Shiv: “Hey Dev, did Khan pick up his phone?”

Dev: “No, man. He didn’t.”

Mayank: “What happened?”

Dev: “Khan is not picking up his phone. I have been trying a lot.”

Mayank: “Mota must be sleeping, I am damn sure. Don’t worry.”

Dev: “I hope you are right.”

Suddenly, Dev’s phone rang. It was Khan. Dev picked up quickly and said, “Where are you, man? Why the bloody hell have you not been picking up your phone?”

“Hey, Dev. Actually, the phone was on silent mode,” Khan said in a dull and heavy voice.

“What happened, bro? Is everything alright?”

“Yeah, dude. Everything is fine,” Khan said, but with very low energy again.

“You don’t sound like it. Where are you right now? Come here, we are having so much fun.”

“I cannot, I am at the hospital.”

“Hospital!? What are you doing there? What happened, bro? Tell me honestly,” replied a shocked Dev.

There was no reply from the other side. Dev insisted again, “Bhai, what happened? Which hospital are you in? What happened, are you alright?”

No voice came from the other side. Dev had come away from the group while talking to Khan.

Khan was absolutely silent. No sound came from his side for a while. Suddenly, he heard him sobbing on the other side. Yes, Khan was sobbing. Dev got even more worried. “What happened, dude?”

“Bhai, Mummy…”

“What happened to your mum?”

“Bhai, she’s in the ICU.”

“What the fuck? Where are you, man? Which hospital?”

“Sahara,” he said and disconnected the call.

Dev got so worried that tears started to roll down his too eyes. He dropped Khan a message on WhatsApp, “Bhai, I am coming.”

CHAPTER EIGHT

Mayank, Dev and Shiv made their way to Sahara Hospital in Gomtinagar. It was the time of the evening rush hour when people left from their offices to go home, and the traffic was very high.

Dev was lost deep in his thoughts. His first memory of Khan became fresh in his mind.

Dev was being dropped to school by his driver. He was feeling quite happy about going to school for the first time, as all his friends in his colony used to go to school, while he was home-schooled by tutors who used to come to his house and teach him.

He used to feel very lonely at home after his elder brother and every other child in the neighbourhood left for school each morning. It was difficult for him to pass the time till noon. After a lot of tantrums then, he was finally admitted to a school. Dev was being led by his driver into the school. There, at the gate of the building, he saw a very cute, chubby and innocent looking Khan, crying profusely against going to school. He was accompanied by his mom. Each time his mom tried to send him in with the watchman, he just ran back to her. When Khan did not stop crying, Khan's mom pointed to Dev and said, "Look, he is also going to school, but he is not crying at all. Why are you crying then, beta? You will have fun here." Khan's mom pointed towards Dev again and said to Dev, "Beta, take him along with you."

It was since then that Khan and Dev had been friends. Dev knew of Khan's attachment towards his mom. He was not able to figure out what had happened. All he knew was that the most important person in Khan's life was his mom.

Mayank was sitting quietly, trying to console his mind that nothing wrong was going to happen. He knew that whatever the case maybe, and however much he and Khan teased each other, they both were best buddies.

Shiv was in absolute shock, as he had always only heard about the ICU, but had never been to one before. All he knew was that if a person was in an ICU, the situation must be critical. He silently prayed to his dear Bajrang Bali for nothing bad to happen, and for things to be alright.

Usually, it did not take more than twenty minutes to reach Gomtinagar, but due to the heavy traffic, it took them more than 50 minutes to get to the town and another fifteen minutes to reach the hospital. Rakesh parked the car.

Dev and Mayank entered the hospital, followed by Shiv. Khan was not picking up his phone now.

They reached the ICU, but there was no one there from Khan's family. Shiv first thought that perhaps Khan had been kidding about the whole thing, but on a second thoughts, it seemed ridiculous for Khan to joke about such a thing. But then, why was there no one at the Hospital?

Dev looked around, only to find a compounder there.

"Bhaiya, was there someone in the ICU now?"

"Now? No, there was no one here now."

"I mean, was there an aunty in the ICU earlier today?"

"Are you talking about the Khan family?"

"Yes, yes exactly!"

"Arrey baba, they are such nice people. I don't know how God could do this to them. Both her sons were so shattered when they got to know the news. It should not have happened to her at such an early age."

"What happened exactly?"

"Arrey, you don't know? She had cancer and now she is no more. She passed away nearly half an hour ago."

***

Khan, Mayank, Dev and Shiv were at Indira Dam.

Indira Dam was a dam on the outskirts of Lucknow. There were never too many people there. Dev and Khan had been going there since class 9th.

It was a quiet place without much people or noise. Sitting at such a place, only the sound of the flowing water and birds could be heard which calmed the mind.

It was just as peaceful that day, but it was not calming their minds at all.

Khan was the first to break the silence.

Looking at the river and avoiding everyone's eye, he said, "Bhai, I should not have drank beer today. What happened to my mom was all because of that. My mom was in the hospital when I reached there in a drunken state. She had cancer, last stage. It was bound to happen, but who had expected that she would leave me alone in this world so early. I never had even the slight knowledge of her disease."

"Bhai, you couldn't have done anything. It's just not in our hands, bhai." Dev was trying to console Khan, but he knew that nothing was going to help at that time.

"Bhai, I will never ever touch beer or any other thing again."

Dev simply hugged Khan. Mayank and Shiv hugged them too.

Dev, Mayank and Shiv: "Bhai, we will always be there for you."

Mayank: "Bhai, we do not have any control over life or death."

Khan was still not in his senses. He just had tears in his eyes.

Shiv was still not able to accept this. He had a lot of different things on his mind.

What control does anyone have over life?

'Everyone talks about Karma? But what is the difference between destiny and karma? Can anyone change his destiny with his karma? If yes, then how? Whose fault was it in Khan's mom's death? Who should be held responsible for it?' Shiv was unable to figure these questions out and these thoughts continues to buzz in his mind.

He was totally shocked upon hearing of such a sudden death. 'Does death always come so suddenly? Why do people plan anything, when they are not even certain about the very next moment of their life? In this case, it was a disease. What control does anyone have over diseases or accidents? If a man has to get his son/daughter married or support his family, but he dies suddenly in an accident or acquires an incurable disease, what can he possibly do? How can one take care of these things? Is there any possible solution for such situations?'

There was a character in Mahabharata called Eklavya who worked very hard to master the art of archery, but it only took seconds for Dronacharya to ask him to cut his thumb off as his fee. Why did this happen? Was this his fate? If this was his fate indeed, then what was the use of practising day and night to master archery?

Did he master archery only to cut his thumb off at the end? Had he not cut his thumb off, perhaps he would have become a more fierce and mighty warrior than Arjuna himself. Only time has the answer to all such questions.

• • •

CHAPTER NINE

The day of the exams arrived and the first paper was that of Maths. Shiv was waiting for others at the tea stall in front of the school. He had just received a call from Luv.

Luv was about to reach the school entrance in ten minutes. Luv had got special permission from the principal to be allowed to sit for the exams directly without having attended any classes. From that point of view, it was his first day at school. Khan, on the other hand, had not been the same guy since his mom passed away.

He has become very serious in his attitude and had started accompanying his father to work. He limited his socialising to a great extent. It had been more than a week since Shiv saw him last.

"Hey Shiv," Luv approached him from across the road, carrying a bag on his back.

"Hi, Luv. How are you?"

"I am fine, how about you?"

"I am also good. So, all set for the exam?"

"Yeah, I am well prepared, and you?"

"Well, I won't say very well prepared. I have just gone through all the formulas and theorems."

"That's good."

"Hey Luv, I will introduce you to my friends."

"Okay."

"There is this one friend of mine, Khan, who lost his mother just last month, so don't mind if he acts a little weirdly."

"Oh, I am so sorry to hear that. What happened, man?"

"Oh, it was cancer."

"Oh.."

"By the way, how have you come?"

"On my bike."

"Oh, that's cool. Which bike do you have?"

"I have a Super Splendor. It is fast, man."

"Hahahaha, did you just say 'Super Splendor'?" Mayank entered the conversation just then.

Shiv: "Hey, Maya. Ssup!"

Mayank: "I am cool, man. How are you?"

Shiv: "So am I. Meet Luv, he is a family friend and is a new admission to our section too."

Mayank: "Hi, Luv."

Luv: "Hi, Mayank"

Mayank: "Did he just say that he came on a Super Splendor?"

Shiv: "Yeah, he just did." He gestured at Mayank to not make mockery out of his bike.

Mayank: "It is a nice bike, actually."

The roaring sound of another bike just then announced the arrival of Dev and Khan together.

Dev: "Hey, guys. Ssup! All prepared for the exam?"

Mayank: “Yo man! I am ever ready for any exam.”

He signalled towards his pockets and said, “Dude, I have all the theorems and formulas right here in my pocket. I spend three hours making them last night.”

Dev: “You still use handmade chits? Come on, dude. Make use of technology. Look, I have got reductions of all the theorems and formulas here. The best part is, I have five copies of all of them, in case anyone needs it.”

Mayank: “What the fuck, man? Show me, what have you got?”

Mayank took those reductions from Dev. They were zerox copies of book pages reduced to $1/5^{th}$ of their original size, to make them easy to hide. Luv was shocked. He had never seen such cheating methods in his life. In fact, he had never even cheated in his life.

“Don’t you guys fear?” said a surprised Luv.

Dev: “Fear from whom? By the way, who are you?”

Shiv: “Hey guys, this is Luv. A family friend of mine and a new plus late admission to our class.”

Dev: “Okay, hi Luv. I am Dev, and dude, there is no chance of us getting caught. I have a lot of experience, so there is nothing to fear. In case you need some, you can have it too.”

Luv: “Oh, no no, thanks a lot, bro. I don’t need them.”

Khan: “As you wish.”

Shiv: “Hey, Khan. How have you been? All set for the exam?”

Khan: “Hey, I have been good. Yeah, I am all set, the same way as Dev. I am not prepared well, but it does not mean that I am going to cheat. Dude, in case I get caught, I can’t even imagine what will happen.”

Shiv: “That’s good. I am not going to try that thing either. It is good for Mayank and Dev only. All the best, guys. Let’s get in.”

Dev and Mayank started stuffing their chits in their socks and tie and other hiding places. They all entered the school together.

***

When the final bell rang after the exam, everyone started pouring out of the hall. Mayank and Dev seemed quite happy. Yet, it was difficult to judge how it went for them, since they were always happy.

Shiv was not satisfied with the way his paper had gone, but that did not seem to be the case with Luv. He seemed quite satisfied with his exam.

Dev: “Hey guys, Ssup? How was your paper?”

Shiv: “Mine was not so good.”

Mayank: “All the questions they asked were numerical, man. Not a single theorem based question. I was only able to use my formula’s chit.”

Khan: “I am just wondering why everyone took so many extra sheets for the paper. I wasn’t even able to finish the first sheet, which too I filled mostly by writing down the questions from the question paper itself.”

Shiv went over to Luv and asked, “How did your paper go, Luv?”

“Mine was okay - not so good, not so bad. How was yours?”

“That’s great. Mine was not too good. Actually, it was not satisfactory at all.”

“Oh,” Luv was about to console Shiv, but he was interrupted by a sweet voice.

Priyanka: “Hey, guys. How are you? How was your paper?”

Shiv: “Hi, Priyanka. Oh, it was not satisfactory. How was yours?”

Priyanka: “Mine was good. I think I will score good. Hi, Luv. How are you?”

Luv: “Hi Priyanka, I am good. My paper was also good. I also hope to get good marks.”

Priyanka: “That is great. I am sorry for you, Shiv, I hope you will do better in the upcoming papers.”

Shiv: “I hope that too. Hey guys, I will catch you later. I just saw a friend of mine and I need to go. Bye.”

Priyanka: “Bye, Shiv.”

Luv: “Dude, call me when you are free?”

Shiv: “Sure, I will.”

Shiv spotted Prateek chatting with some friends near the boundary wall.

“Hey, Prateek. How was your exam?”

“Mine was good, how was yours?”

“Mine wasn’t quite that good. I hadn’t practiced enough. By the way, can I get your physics notebook? I need the notes.”

“If I give you my notes, how will I study, bro?”

“I mean, I will get them photocopied.”

“But I have not brought that notebook with me today.”

“Hmm. Can we go to your house and get that done?”

“Yeah, sure. We can do that, but I am not going home straightaway right now. I have to attend a few coaching classes. Can you come down to my place in the evening at 4 PM?”

“Great, I will be there. It’s not an issue. Thanks, bro.”

• • •

"Okay, see you then."

Shiv took out his phone and called Luv.

"Where are you, Luv?"

"I am right there where you left us."

"'Us?' You mean, you are still there with Priyanka?"

"Yeah, we are just chatting here."

"Dude, I am leaving for home and I will be out in the evening to get some notes on physics from a friend of mine. In case you need the notes too, we can go there together."

"Oh, thank you, bro, but I don't need them. I already have many notes."

"Okay then, I am leaving for home, see you later."

Shiv now called Dev, "Where are you, man?"

"I am here, near Study Hall School."

"What are you doing there?"

"Nothing much, Khan and I are just hanging around. Where are you?"

"I was near the tea stall. Okay then, see you tomorrow."

"Why tomorrow? Wait for 5 minutes, we will be there. Call Mayank also."

"Okay."

As Dev had promised, he and Khan arrived at the tea stall in the next five minutes. Mayank reached there too.

Mayank: "What fun have you both been having lately?"

Khan: "We were just hanging around near Study Hall, searching for our Bhabhi."

Shiv: "Bhabhi? Which one?"

Dev: “Dude, that Study Hall one. The one we saw during the match.”

Shiv: “Oh yes, yes, did you find her?”

Khan: “No, dude. We’ve only managed to find out her name and class yet. Her name is Geetika Pant and she is a student of class 11 too. Just wait for a few more days, our detective Romeo Dev will definitely find out everything else about her, hahahaha.”

Mayank: “Hahaha, I just hope he doesn’t join the DEVDAS group.”

Dev: “Don’t worry, bro. I will not join that DEVDAS group.”

Mayank and Khan started teasing Dev about his new-found interest. It seemed like Khan had finally started to get over his mom’s death. At least, it appeared to be so.

***

The Nokia tune played loud on Shiv’s phone. It was Dev. Shiv looked at his watch, it was 3:30 PM by his watch. He was getting ready to leave for Prateek’s house.

“Yeah, Dev?”

“Where are you, bro?”

“I am at home, and you?”

“I am also at your home. Come out.”

“Wait a minute.”

Shiv came out of his house and saw a white Swift, numbered ‘7766’ and fitted with a blue beacon on top. On top of the number plate, it was written, ‘UTTAR PRADESH GOVERNMENT’.

“Get in, Shiv. Let’s go.”

“What are you doing here?”

“Nothing, just passing my time.”

“Is this your car?”

“Yeah. By the way, were you going somewhere?”

“Actually, I was going to get some notes from Prateek.”

“Pratee? That shy guy from our class?”

“Yes.”

“Let’s go then, Where is his house?”

“Indra-nagar.”

Dev drove off towards Prateek’s house. Shiv had sat in red beacon’d cars before, but never in a blue one. Blue beacons symbolised administration, while the red beacons were reserved only for the ministers. This was first time that he was sitting in a blue beacon’d car.

“Dev, why have you never taken your car out before?”

“Actually, dude, my brother left for his college just yesterday. When he is in Lucknow, he uses the car and I have to use the bike, but now since he has gone away to his college, both the things are mine, hehehe.”

“Hahahaha, cool!”

Prateek had already SMSed his exact address to Shiv, so it did not take them much time to reach there. Prateek’s house was that of an average middle class family, There was a small veranda out front, where a Maruti Alto was parked.

Prateek came out of his house, wearing half pants and a white undervest. He was also carrying a notebook in his hand. Shiv got out of the car and went to Prateek. Dev said a formal hello while reversing his car to head back.

“Here it is. How long are you going to take?”

"Exactly the amount of time that the shopkeeper takes to photostat it. Not more that that."

"Okay."

"You can come along if you wish."

"No, bro. Thanks, I have got to study."

"Okay."

Shiv went back to sit in the car and they drove off. They searched for the nearest photo-copy shop and gave the register to the shopkeeper. Dev parked near a pan shop and bought a cigarette and Rajnigandha. A song from Aashiqui 2, 'Tum hi ho', was playing in the background.

Dev started making rings of smoke. Shiv tried to copy him. Dev suddenly said, "Bhai, this song is awesome, na?"

"Yeah, dude, it is. It has become so popular these days."

"Dude, her face just doesn't get off my mind."

"Whose face? Geetika's?"

"Yeah, bro. I am just unable to stop my mind from going in that direction."

"Are you serious?"

"Yes, bro. I am absolutely serious. She seems to be the cutest beauty I have ever seen in my life. I am unable to forget her innocent face. I think I am in love, bro. This has never happened before. I came to your place today because I got to know that she stays somewhere over there."

"Dude, are you sure it is love? It could just be infatuation, like I had for Ishani."

"I don't think it's just infatuation. I have never had feelings like this before, bro. I have always been the least interested in girls, but with this girl, I just hope something happens between us, bro."

"Well, nothing is going to happen until and unless you do something."

"But, what should I do and how?"

"Hmm...something has to be done, bro. Otherwise, nothing will happen. You have to give in some input in order to get an output."

"Dude, stop talking like a computer teacher. Try being a love guru for the moment."

"Okay, we will sort this out after the exams."

"Okay, okay, after the exams, as you say. I think you should go and pick up your notes. They must have been done by now."

"Hmm..."

Shiv took the notes from the shop after paying the amount to the shopkeeper. They headed back to Prateek's house. It hardly took them five minutes to reach there.

A royal blue Bajaj scooter was parked in front of Prateek's house and an elderly person was standing there. Shiv did not take much time to recognise him as Prateek's father, since they resembled each other a lot.

Prateek's father was wearing a white shirt with blue stripes and a black trouser below. It seemed as if he had just returned from his office. He seemed puzzled to see a blue beacon'd car stopping in front of his house.

Shiv came out and greeting 'Namaste' to uncle and requested him to call Prateek. He gave them a weird look, first to Shiv and then to Dev still sitting in the car. He then called Prateek.

Prateek came out and seemed quite hesitant. He avoided talking to them much. He just took his note book and went inside his house as soon as possible. Dev noticed this behaviour, but didn't utter a word.

• • •

Shiv and Dev turned the car around and were off, raising a lot of dust behind.

Prateek's dad went inside the house, closed the door, called Prateek and asked, "Who was that guy?"

"Papa, his name is Shiv. He is in my class."

"What did he come here for?"

"Papa, he had missed some classes, so he needed my notes. He had come for that."

"You have your exam tomorrow. How could you give your notes to someone else?"

"Papa, he took the register from me just half an hour ago."

"Don't you have to study?"

"Yes, papa. I do."

"Then why did you give him your notes? Make sure this does not happen again. Keep your friends' business limited to your school. Don't bring them home."

"Okay, papa."

"What does his father do?"

"Papa, his father is an MLA."

"MLA, a politician?" Prateek did not know that this answer would double his father's anger.

"Yes, papa," said a fear-stricken Prateek.

"You know these politicians are a fraud. You should keep your distance from such rich spoiled politician's children. I know how these politicians are. They are not good people and the same goes for their sons. Make sure he doesn't come our way again."

"But papa, he is in my class."

"Then keep your friendship to your class only."

"Okay, papa."

"Now go to your room and study for your exam."

Prateek did not say a word more, but just went to his small room which comprised only of a study table, a bed, a night lamp, an all-out mosquito killer and lots of books everywhere.

Prateek took out his H. C. Verma physics book. He tried hard to concentrate, but was unable to. He had just one thing going on in his mind, what the hell was wrong if someone came and took notes from him? Why is his father always angry with him?

The previous year, he had been thrashed by his father for having scored just 92% in the boards. His father always thought of him as a fool. Prateek knew that there was only one way to get out of this mess, which was by getting admission in an IIT or NIT, but that was no easy task either.

Giving up on his thoughts, Prateek started to focus on his book again.

• • •

CHAPTER TEN

The last day of the exams arrived with the environmental studies paper, which was the easiest paper of all. Diwali holidays were going to start from the next day and school was to remain closed for the next 10 days.

Most students had come without bags, as they all had special plans for the day, after the exam got over. Some had planned for a movie, some had planned to go to ZERO DEGREE (a disco in the city).

In all of this, how could Mayank let himself be left behind.

Mayank had been sitting at the tea stall for more than ten minutes and Dev had still not arrived. He had told him that he would be there in five minutes. He was usually never late.

Mayank was about to call him again when he heard a siren (as one of an ambulance). Mayank turned around only to find Dev playing that siren on his Swift. Dev, Shiv and Khan were already inside. Khan rolled down his window and asked Mayank to get in.

Mayank: “Wassup, Khan bhai?”

Khan: “The usual.”

Mayank: “So Dev, where are we going, man?”

Shiv: “We will just go and take a round near Study Hall, smoke a cigarette, and be back for the exam.”

Mayank: “Okay.”

Dev: “So, Mayank bhai, what is the plan after the exam?”

Mayank: “First of all, don’t call me Mayank.”

Everyone: “Why, bro? What happened?”

Mayank: “Because now, my name is ‘Sultan Mirza’.”

Shiv: “‘Sultan Mirza’ from ‘Once Upon a Time in Mumbai’?”

Mayank: “Yeah, that’s the one. I saw that movie on TV just yesterday. Amazing movie, bro. I regret not having watched it in a theatre.”

Everyone shouting loudly, “Okay, SULTAN bhai.”

Mayank: “Yeah, and as far as today’s plan is concerned, we are going to have a blast in the exam and after that, we will have beer and then go for a movie.”

Dev: “Blast? What blast?” He lit a cigarette.

Mayank: “How can we have a Diwali break without having a blast at school? Hahahaha.” Saying this, Mayank opened his bag and took out three cracker bombs.

Shiv: “Dude, what is this?”

Khan: “These are desi bombs. Where did you get them, Sultan bhai?”

Mayank: “Bhai, I just asked my servant to get a few for me.”

Shiv: “And what are these sticks on them?”

Mayank: “These are incense sticks, the ones which we use at our homes for pooja.”

Shiv: “What are they for?”

Mayank: “These are the timers.”

Shiv: “Timers? What do they do?”

Mayank: “Look, the thread is tied to the bottom of the stick. Until the stick burns all the way to the bottom, the bomb is not going to explode. It will give us enough time to go back and sit in our classes and and when the bomb finally explodes after ten minutes, no one will be able to point a finger at us. Understood?”

Dev: “Hahahaha, nice Jugaad, bhai.”

Shiv: “Yeah man, it is a nice one. Where will we put all these?”

Mayank: “One in boys’ toilet, one in Girls’ toilet and one in the staff toilet. What do you say, guys?”

Khan: “It is a great plan, man. Just make sure that no one gets hurt.”

Mayank: “One for me, one for Dev, and one?”

Khan: “Shiv, who else?”

Mayank: “Okay, so it is decided. Boys, let’s celebrate Diwali.”

Everyone: “HAPPY DIWALI!”

***

Five minutes had passed since the exam started, but three guys were still missing from the class. Khan was sitting on his chair, wondering why Mayank, Dev and Shiv had not reached the class yet.

Shiv and Mayank were returning after having planted bombs in the staff toilet. “Everything is done now, let’s just get back to our class as soon as we can,” suggested Mayank.

“I will be right back, after checking things at our toilet.”

“Do not worry about that, Dev has gone there. Everything will be alright.”

“But he is all alone, man. Let me go and have a look.”

“As you wish. I am going to the class. I am going to give the excuse of a bike puncture, so do not use that excuse when you come by, okay?”

“Dude, this is not done at all, man. You always take the easiest ones.”

“Fuck off!” said Mayank and showed his middle finger to Shiv. He went back to his class with a wicked smile on his face.

Shiv went to the toilet. Hearing footsteps outside Dev rushed out of the toilet.

“Hey D…” Before Shiv could complete his sentence, Dev signalled at him to maintain silence. Shiv came closer to him and asked what was going on.

Dev signalled him again to keep calm and took him inside the toilet. They both entered the last compartment where Dev had planted both his bombs. Dev signalled Shiv to go closer to the wall and listen.

Shiv put his ear to the wall and started listening. He could hear some whispers coming from the other side of the wall. There was a female voice and a male voice.

MV: "Oh come on, please, just once."

FV: "Let's go back to our classes. We have an exam."

MV: "When have I asked you to stay here all day?"

FV: *laughing sound*

MV: "But please, one French kiss."

FV: "No baba, we have an exam."

MV: "You talk as if we have never kissed each other before. What happened at your house when I came over for group study?"

FV (aggressively): "What happened that day? Nothing happened. You were the one begging for a kiss and you were the one who brought that basket full of Ferrero Rochers."

MV (trying to calm the other): "So, I am the one asking today as well. As for the chocolates, I will buy you lots more after the exam."

Shiv whispered in Dev's ear, "Let's go back to our class, or everyone will think that we planted this bomb."

"Everyone is going to think that anyway, brother," Dev replied.

"Still, I insist."

"Okay, if you insist."

• • •

Shiv and Dev came out of the toilet and started walking towards their class.

"What the hell was happening in there?" asked a curious Shiv.

"Bhai, something has been going on there for the past 5 minutes."

"Who were these two?"

"How will I know, bro? But I can guess that they are either from ninth or eleventh standard as these two are the only classes that have an exam today."

"What were they talking about?"

"You can listen to it yourself after the exam," said Dev and pointed towards his phone.

"You son of a bitch, you recorded that conversation?"

"You can abuse me as much as you can, but only after I upload this file to our school's confession page on Facebook."

"Hahahaha. By the way, did you ask everyone to shout Happy Diwali the moment the bombs explode?"

"Oh yeah, bro, do not worry about that."

Dev and Shiv entered the class. They saw Mayank and Khan present there already. After taking permission from the teacher, they walked in and took their respective seats. Dev showed a victory sign to Khan, who was made to sit on the first bench that day.

There was pin drop silence in this class, as well as all the other classes. Shiv's heartbeat rose.

• • •

Mayank was sweating heavily. Dev was expecting to hear a BANG sound any moment. Khan's hands were near his ears, to close them the moment it heard a loud sound.

Boom went the first cracker and everyone shouted, "HAPPY DIWAALI!"

The teachers were so surprised, they didn't know what to do. They started moving here and there, trying to understand what had just happened. Hardly a minute had passed when the second bomb went off with a loud bang as well.

This one was much louder than the first one. There was also the sound of a loud scream accompanying this bang.

***

"Ma'am, can I please take a minute." The coordinator entered the class and asked this of the invigilator.

"Sure, sir."

"A boy has been injured due to this naughty act. I don't know who has done this, but I will make sure that the culprit is expelled from the school today itself. That boy is bleeding, we've made him sit in the staff room. Do these people have any idea of what they have done? I am not going to spare anyone. Who are the prefects in this class?"

A very horrified Mudit Sinha stood up at his seat.

"Mudit, you are one of the senior prefects present here. Go along with the other prefects and announce in each and every class that either the culprits come to my cabin themselves, or I am going to expel each and every student present here today."

"Okay, sir."

"This time, the students have gone way too far. I will not spare them." Saying this, he left the class and went to his cabin.

A horrified Mudit went out of the class and started doing what he had been commanded to do. The invigilator started talking to the invigilator from the next section, standing at the door.

Mayank: "Is it true, what the coordinator said?"

Shiv: "I knew something was going to go wrong."

Dev: "Guys, I am not able to understand one thing."

Mayank: "What?"

Dev: "What the fuck happened to the third one?"

"Hahahaha!" Khan caught everyone's attention with his loud laughter.

"Shh, no talking," the Invigilator tried to control the class.

Mayank: "Bro, you are still worried about the third bomb? I am wondering who the boy is who got hurt?"

Dev: "Dude, everyone was busy with the paper. There couldn't have been anyone in the toilet. The coordinator is bluffing so that we confess ourselves. There can't be anyone there, yaar."

Shiv: "But, what if there indeed was someone there?"

Dev: "Bhai, our class is just next to the toilet. Guys, I just want to say that if anyone went to the toilet, he would have had to cross our door. I have been paying attention ever since I entered the class this morning, and believe me, no one went to the toilet."

Shiv: “What if someone was already there in the toilet, what then?”

Dev: “Bhai, we were the last ones to leave the toilet. No one was there, remember?”

Shiv: “You try to remember, bhai. There was definitely someone there while we were there.”

Dev: “Oh, fuck! Yes, you are right, bro. There was definitely someone there. But they were two people there. How can only the boy get injured?”

Mayank: “What the hell are you guys talking about?”

Dev: “Bhai, someone was there in the girls’ toilet when we were there.”

Mayank: “In the girls’ toilet? What would someone be doing there?”

Dev: “Bhai, there was a couple there. I have recorded their conversation.”

Mayank: “But they said that only a boy got injured. What happened to the girl?”

Dev: “That is what I am not able to understand.”

Mayank: “Look there, Mudit is back. Let me ask him who the boy is.”

He called him, “Hey, Mudit. What happened, man? Who’s the boy that got injured?”

“He is some new admission to our school, some Chaudhary.”

CHAPTER ELEVEN

It was Diwali time and everyone was busy with some work or the other. Rakesh was busy cleaning the house with the others. Shiv had had breakfast. Shiv's mom was busy making preparations for the evening pooja of Goddess Lakshmi and Lord Ganesh.

"Mom, where is Dad?"

"He has gone to meet some bureaucrats and other officers for Diwali."

"Okay."

It had been only four days since the incident at school. It could be called sheer luck that nobody was harmed grievously at school, and that the school was closing for vacations the same day.

There was also no evidence against anyone, or all four of them would have been punished severely.

Shiv hadn't met Luv since that incident. He tried calling him a few times but his phone was out of reach. Thus, on Diwali, Shiv decided to go to Luv's place and meet him.

"Hey Rakesh, do you know Luv's address?"

"Which Luv, bhaiya?"

"Arrey, I mean that Chaudhary sahab's address?"

"Yes, bhaiya ji. I know it. His house is right behind Eram Girls' Degree College."

"Okay, thanks."

"Are you going there, bhaiya ji?"

"Yes, I am going there."

"Alone?"

"Yes, alone. Can I leave now, Rakesh?"

"Okay, bhaiya ji."

Shiv drove off in his car. It was quite early in the morning, so there wasn't much rush on the roads. It hardly took him fifteen minutes to reach Luv's place.

There was a park next to the lane behind Eram Girls' College and all the houses there were built surrounding this park. There was not one empty plot there. The house right in front of the park's entry had a name plate with 'R.P. Chaudhary, Minister, Uttar Pradesh Government' written on it.

Shiv parked his car in front of the house, stepped out and went to ring the doorbell.

A man wearing an undervest came out and said, "Yes, what do you want?"

"Is Luv home? I am his friend, Shiv. Can you please call him?" Shiv asked him politely.

The man opened the gate to the plot right next to the house and asked Shiv to come inside. He then opened the door of a room there and asked Shiv to have a seat there and wait, while he called Luv.

Shiv took a seat on the sofa in that room. There was a centre table, a bed, a TV and a washbasin in the room. There was also another room attached to it. There were a few framed photographs of Luv's father on the wall.

• • •

Luv didn't take much time to arrive. He was wearing trousers and a tailor made shirt.

"Hey, Shiv. How are you brother? Happy Diwali."

"Hey, Happy Diwali, brother. I am good. How are you?"

"I am also good. How come you paid me a visit and how did you find my house?"

"We hadn't met at all since the Diwali holidays started and your phone was not reachable too, so I thought I would come pay you a visit."

"Oh. Actually, my phone fell in the washing machine, so it is not working. I also lost all my contacts so I wasn't able to inform anyone." Before Luv finished this statement, that man in the undervest came in with a tray in hand. It had some sweets and two glass of water on it.

"Arrey, there is no need for such formalities, brother," Shiv expressed his gratitude.

"No formalities, bro, it's Diwali. How can we have Diwali without sweets and crackers. This is Chotu, our helping hand at home."

"Okay, Happy Diwali, Chotu bhaiya," Shiv wished him with a smile.

"Bhaiya ji, aapko bhi Happy Diwali," said Chotu and went inside the house.

"So, brother, do you remember what happened that day at school?"

"Oh, bro! How can I ever forget that day? I was unable to hear from my left ear for the entire day. I am thankful to God that it was only temporary and that I got better the very next day."

"Oh…thank God." Shiv thought it wise to keep his mouth shut regarding the particular situation. Showing as if he was completely oblivious to the situation, Shiv asked, "What exactly happened on that unfortunate day?"

"Bhai, I had just gone to pee in the toilet. I was already late for the exam and I was in a hurry. The moment I went to the washbasin to wash my hands, there was a loud BOOM behind me. I only felt the bang in my ear and after that, I was unable to hear anything else. The bang sound continued to ring in my ear for a long time."

"Shit! Then what happened, brother?"

"Nothing, the teachers came in and took me to the staffroom. From there, I was sent home. Nothing serious happened and I am really thankful to God for that."

"Hmm. So, is everything okay now?"

"Yeah, bro. I am fine and everything is great now."

"That's great. What are you doing in the evening today?"

"No idea. I will most probably be free after the pooja."

"Okay. I will come here in the evening after the pooja then and we will celebrate Diwali together, okay?"

"That sounds good, see you then."

***

Mayank was standing at Dev's main gate. He rang the bell. Dev shouted, "Just a minute."

He came out wearing a jeans, a casual shirt and a pair of slippers. This was his usual choice of clothes, whether it was a special occasion or not.

"Bhai, a very happy and prosperous Diwali to you," Mayank shouted the moment he saw Dev.

"Bhai, a very happy and prosperous Diwali to you too," Dev replied.

"Oh ho, is this your new Endeavour?"

"Yes, bhai."

"White colour suits you, man. This SUV definitely goes with the personality, Sultan bhai," Dev said and laughed out loud.

"Thank you, bhai."

"Let's check the top speed."

"Sure, bhai," Mayank said and tossed the keys to Dev.

Dev unlocked the car and took the driver's seat, while Mayank went to sit next to him.

"So, Dev bhai, where shall we go first?"

"Hmm, let's first get Khan, then Shiv, then we shall celebrate Diwali."

"Okay, then."

Dev made the engine roar and headed towards Khan's house. Mayank lit two cigarettes, one for himself and one for Dev.

"Thanks, bro. Do one thing, call Khan and ask him to come out of his house."

"Okay," said Mayank and dialled Khan.

"A very happy and prosperous Diwali to you and your family, Khan bhai."

"Thank you, and to you and your family too, Mayank bhai."

"Dev bhai is also saying Happy Diwali to you, man."

"Bhai, tell him I wish him the same."

"Come out of your house and do it yourself."

• • •

"You asshole, couldn't you have said it before that you are standing outside? Wait a minute," said Khan and disconnected the call.

"Dev bhai, he is coming in a minute."

"We will also take just a minute or two to reach his place."

Khan came out of his house to find nobody there. With the thought of abusing Mayank for being late, he took out his phone, but before he could dial the number, he saw two big headlights approaching him. They came to a halt right next to Khan.

Dev: "Khan bhai, get in fast."

Khan: "A very happy Diwali to both my brothers."

Mayank: "Happy Diwali to you too, bhai."

Khan opened the front door and said, "Mayank bhai, if you don't mind, please sit behind, yaar. I get headaches sitting in the back."

"Not an issue at all, Khan bhai," said Mayank and went to the backseat.

Khan: "So, where now?"

Dev: "Let's go to Shiv's place."

Khan: "Yeah, let's pick him up, but where is his house?"

Dev: "Why the hell do you worry when you already have a driver who knows all the directions and you don't even have to pay him."

Khan: "Yes, exactly. Why the hell should I worry? Anyway, Mayank bhai, how is Aradhana bhabhi?"

Mayank: "Oh, she is great. She has gone to her uncle's house for a family get together."

Khan: "Okay, Sultan bhai…"

Dev: "Bhai, call Shiv and ask him to come out too."

Mayank: "Yeah, sure I will."

He took out his phone and dialled Shiv's number.

"Bro, he is not picking up his phone," Mayank said after a few seconds.

"Not picking? Okay, then let's go to his house straightaway," said Khan, while busy on WhatsApp with some girl.

Dev: "Whom are you chatting with on WhatsApp so seriously? Who on this earth has got your interest?"

Khan: "You better drive, Mr. Driver. It is none of your business. By the way, it is not WhatsApp. I am using 'We Chat'." He finished with a mischievous tone.

Dev: "We Chat? The one whose advertisement features Varun Dhawan and Parineeti Chopra?"

Khan: "Yeah, the same one, and you know…."

Before Khan could complete his sentence, his phone was snatched away from his hands by Mayank.

"What nonsense is this Mayank Verma? Bloody asshole, return my phone!" Khan commanded furiously. He became really angry by this act of Mayank.

"I will definitely, but only after I see the picture of whom you are talking to," said Mayank in a teasing tone. "Whoa! This girl is hot, man. How did you get this girl?" asked a shocked Mayank.

"What happened? Which hot girl are you guys talking about? Show me too," Dev said, curious to see her picture.

"Arrey, we have reached Shiv's place. Look, he is placing 'diyas' next to the gate," Khan pointed towards the front of Shiv's house.

Shiv had on a traditional white kurta and pyjama. There was also another guy there, standing right next to him. Dev parked the car and everyone alighted from it.

Dev, Khan and Mayank said all together, “Shiv bhai, a very happy and prosperous Diwali to you and your family.”

Shiv: “Bhai, to you all too.”

Mayank approached closer and noticed the other guy standing next to Shiv. “Arrey, Luv bhai, you are here too! A very happy Diwali to you.”

“Guys, same to all of you,” replied a modest Luv.

“Oh, Luv bhai is also here. Happy Diwali, bhai,” said Dev and shook hands with Luv.

“To you also, bhai,” Luv replied.

Khan: “Shiv, let’s go, man.”

Shiv: “Where?”

Dev: “Arrey, we will just take a round, munna.”

Shiv: “Okay, let’s go.”

CHAPTER TWELVE

Aaaja tujhe bhi main kara dun,

Tamanche pe Disco,

Tamanche pe Disco,

Tamanche pe Disco…

The boys were busy doing 'disco on Tamancha' in the car. Dev was driving the car, while Khan was sitting beside him. Shiv, Mayank and Luv were sitting in the rear seat.

The festival of Diwali, which is also known as the festival of light, symbolises the defeat of evil and the victory of right over wrong. Each and every house was decorated with lights and 'deep-malas'.

The sound of crackers was at its peak, which was also contributing to air and noise pollution.

Shiv: "So guys, what next?"

Mayank: "What's next, what? Let's get some snacks for 'chakhna', some cold drinks and soda for ourselves."

Dev: "Yooo, that's the spirit, my boy."

Shiv: "Oh God, Mayank has become a drunkard."

Mayank: "No, I am not. It is an occasion, guys. It's Diwali and having drinks on Diwali and playing cards has always been the tradition, guys. It brings good luck."

Khan: “Whatever. I am not going to have even a sip of whatever you’re having.”

Mayank: “Oh, come on, Khan. I have brought you guys Jack Daniels, man.”

Dev: “Is it really J.D.?”

Khan: “What the hell is this J.D. that you guys are talking about? What is it?”

Mayank: “It is among the best scotches made in the world. It is the best, guys.”

At this, Khan, Shiv and Luv said together, “I have never had scotch.”

Dev: “Even I have never had it before, but this is the time, na. Trust me on this, this is the moment when all of us will be tasting scotch together for the first time in our life. It is a very costly scotch, and imported too. Do you guys really want to waste Mayank’s 3,500 bucks?”

Luv: “What? Does it really cost 3,500 rupees?”

Dev: “Yes, my dear. It is really a very costly one.”

After saying this, Dev parked the car in front of a grocery store where they could find their stuff. “Now, Shiv and Luv will go and get snacks, cold drinks, soda and disposable glasses. Khan will go and get the cigarettes, a lighter and Rajnigandha. Mayank will take out the bottle and I will reverse the car. Get to work, everyone,” said Dev hastily.

Shiv, Luv and Khan got down from the car and went to the grocery store. Now, there were only Mayank and Dev in the car.

“So Dev, is it really your first time? I mean, have you never tasted whisky or scotch before?” asked Mayank in a suspicious tone.

"No, bro. I just said that to convince them. Otherwise, these three would never have agreed."

"That is what I thought."

"What about you? And how did you arrange for 3500 rupees to buy a J.D.?"

"Bro this is my first time too. I have never had scotch. As for arranging the money for J.D., I did not buy it."

"You did not buy it. Then? Did you steal it? Mayank Verma, I had never expected this from you."

"Calm down, brother. I did not steal it, man. My brother got this as a gift from someone last to last month and he forgot it in my room. Since then it had been lying there in a gift wrap. Day before yesterday, while I was cleaning my room, I found it and opened the gift wrap to find this."

"What if he comes back asking about it later?"

"He won't. He must have forgotten about it, else he would have taken it from my room long ago. Even if he turns up and asks for it, I will just say that since it was in a gift wrap, I thought it to be a gift item and gifted it to a friend of mine on his birthday."

"Hahahaha, that is a good one. A very valid excuse. By the way, I wanted to tell you something, bhai."

"What?"

"Bro, even I have never tasted this scotch. I have just heard about it from my brother."

"You asshole, you are such a 'kameena', pandit jee."

"Oh, yes I am…hahahaha."

***

Meanwhile, at the grocery store…

"Yeah, make it two peanut masala, one Lays family pack 'Spanish tango flavour'." Shiv was busy buying snacks and other things. Luckily, they had found a store open on the day of the festival.

"Khan bhai, I hope you remember me, Luv. We met on the day of the exam at school. Shiv introduced us."

"Oh yes, Luv bhai. I definitely remember you, brother."

"Bhai, I don't have a positive feeling about this drinking thing, I mean, I have never even had a fruit beer before and these guys are making me drink whisky."

"It is scotch, Luv bhai. It is much better than whisky. Even I am having this for the first time. Believe me, I know everyone present here. I know everyone is having it for the first time."

"Still, bro, I don't know how the hell it will taste. Apart from that, I don't even know what happens after having a drink, but I have definitely heard that people indulge in fights after drinking."

"No, bro, it is not like that. It is all about the amount one takes. If someone drinks more than his capacity then bad things happen, but if one remains well within his limit, he doesn't get drunk."

"And what is the limit, bro?"

"Limit is like, whenever you feel that you are going out of control, you should stop drinking at once and one should never have large pegs. It should be taken in little amounts, I mean small-small pegs. Look, bro, if you eat more than your capacity, you get a loose motion. So is the case with liquor. If you drink more than your capacity, then be ready for the effect after."

"Bro, you talk like you are a professional and drink daily."

"Bro, that is what is called 'confidence'. Hahaha…be cool, enjoy the life."

• • •

"Yeah, you are right. Let's enjoy life, brother."

Shiv had picked up all that they required required. Dev and Mayank were waiting back at the car. Luv was feeling more confident now after getting such 'gyaan' from Khan BABA. Everyone got back in the car.

Dev: "Mayank bhai, start making the pegs, brother."

Mayank had already started his work. He kept five glasses on the dashboard. Dev had parked the car somewhere on the road behind their school.

Mayank opened the bottle, smelled the liquor and said, "Ahaaa." He started pouring the scotch in every glass, making sure that everyone gets an equal amount.

He was making small pegs of 30ml each. Luv, unable to control his curiosity, was the first to ask, "Why is he not filling the glass full? Why is he putting such a less amount in everyone's glass?"

Dev and Mayank started laughing at his innocent question.

"What happened, guys? Why are you all laughing?" asked Luv, making an innocent face again.

Dev: "Brother, I can totally understand your emotions. It happens the first time. Actually, scotch should not be taken directly."

Luv: "Directly? What does that mean?"

Mayank: "It means that we should not drink it directly. I mean, you need to dilute it."

Luv: "But I have seen in so many Amitabh Bachchan movies, where he just opens the bottle and starts drinking from it."

Khan: "Brother, he is Amitabh Bachchan. He can do anything he wants. He is like, 'Rishtey mein toh hum tumhare baap lagte hain, naam hai shahenshah.' But that is a movie, idiot."

Luv: "What happens if we do that?"

Mayank: "Bhai, it will harm your throat and mouth. It is not fruit juice. It is liquor. Now shut your bloody mouth up and watch. You will get the answers to all your questions."

Mayank started adding soda to the glasses. He then added a little amount of coke to them for taste.

The pegs were ready. Mayank passed the pegs on to everyone. Dev asked Shiv to pass a packet of nut cracker to them.

Mayank: "Guys, now we are ready to spoil ourselves with our first pegs of scotch together."

Dev: "Guys, happy Diwali! CHEERS!"

Everyone: "CHEERS, GUYS! HAPPY DIWALI."

Mayank and Dev started gulping down the drink. Shiv, Khan and Luv first saw Mayank and Dev, then they looked at each other and Shiv started drinking. He was in a mood to get it over with quickly so that they could all go home.'

The moment Luv took his first sip and tasted it, he exclaimed, "Yuck! What the hell is this thing? It is so bitter. I am not going to drink this thing."

Mayank and Khan: "You have to finish it."

Mayank and Dev had already finished their first peg, while Shiv had finished nearly half of his glass.

Luv: "Bhai, I cannot drink this. Please, this is very bad in taste."

Mayank: "No brother, you will have to finish this."

Mayank emptied the whole glass forcefully into Luv's mouth.

Before Luv could think anything, an entire glass full of scotch and soda was in his stomach. "Yuck, what the hell!"

Khan gave him 'Lays and said, "Eat it, you will feel better."

Luv took the chips to change the taste of his mouth. "Thanks, Khan. Now I feel better."

Shiv: "Guys, let's go home now."

Mayank: "Who do you think is going to finish the entire bottle? Don't even think about going home so soon, okay?"

Shiv: "Oh, no…"

***

"You know, I have never felt like this. I mean, I just want to get to know her. I just want to tell her that I care, I just want to love her, I just want to spend some quality time with her. I want to be her best friend."

"You should tell her. You should let her know your feelings. Just open up and say everything to her."

"What next? What if she says that she has another boyfriend? What if she says that she is interested in someone else? What if, in short…"

"She rejects you?"

"Yeah, exactly! What if she simply just rejects me? It will be a big problem."

"Then nothing, you'll just have to move on."

"Bro, it is easier said than done. How the bloody hell can she reject me? I just can't handle the thought that she might reject me. I can give her everything, whatever she likes."

"Bro, love is not like that. Love doesn't have a price."

"Dude, come on. Don't start with that lecture of 'Love can't be bought'. I am a strong follower of Emran Hashmi, and believe me, those who say that love can't be bought, they really don't know where to shop for it."

"Oho, 'Jannat'! Hahaha…okay, Dev bhai. As you say."

It seemed as if Dev and Shiv were done with their conversation about love.

Luv and Khan became best buddies by the end of their 3rd peg. Mayank got busy on his phone with his girlfriend; they were finishing some unfinished business.

Everyone was set and high. Mayank returned after finishing his talk. It was 10:00 PM by their watches. Everyone had started to feel drowsy. Dev suddenly jumped at his seat, as if having remembered something.

Dev: "Hey, Luv! Bro, what exactly did you say you were doing in the toilet when that bomb exploded and harmed you?"

Shiv said with a slur in his voice, "He was peeing, he told me."

Dev: "Asshole, if you and I were inside the toilet planting the bomb, then where the hell was he doing 'susu'? In the girls' toilet?"

Mayank and Khan: "Hahaha, eggjactly!"

Luv: "Yes, eggjactly! I was right there."

Dev: "There? Where is this 'there'?"

Luv: "In the girls' toilet, buddy."

Mayank and Khan: "Really? What the fuck were you doing there?"

Dev: "Well, you will get all your answers if you just listen carefully."

Dev connected the aux cable of the car's stereo to his phone and played the recording he had made that day at school. The private conversation between the two voices was not private any longer.

Luv: "Hahahaha, where did you get that, asshole?"

Shiv: "Dev and I were there."

Luv: "Ohkay!"

Mayank: "Cut the crap, just tell us who was the girl that you were hooking up with, that too in the girls' toilet."

Luv: "She is in the commerce section."

Khan: "Who? What is her name?"

Luv: "Priyanka."

Shiv: "Priyanka! Really? You were with her?"

Khan: "Priyanka, who Priyanka?"

Mayank: "Okay, you were not there that day, Khan. That day at the cricket tournament, a hot chick came and talked to Shiv."

Dev: "That girl from the cheerleading team?"

Shiv: "Yes, that one."

Dev: "She is very-very hot, yaar."

Luv: "Oh, yes. She is."

Shiv: "But when and how did all this happen?"

Luv: "Dude, we met at your house only."

Khan: "Don't tell me you impressed her at your first meeting."

Luv: "It was a coincidence then that both of us went to the same teacher for maths tuitions. That is where everything started."

Mayank: "And then?"

Luv: "Then what? Friendship grew and I started going to her house for group study."

Khan: "Come to the point, what all have you done?"

Dev: "Did you? I mean, did you guys get laid?"

Luv: "Oh, no brother. We have only just gone for a movie date and kissed." A smile came to his face as he completed his sentence.

Khan: "Then why the hell are you smiling so much?"

Luv: "No reason, nothing special."

Dev: "Okay, in case you want to keep it a secret, so be it."

Luv: "No, brother. It is not like that."

'Don ka intezaar toh gyarah mulkon ki police kar rahi hai, lekin Don ko pakadna mushkil hi nahi, namumkin hai' Mayank's phone rang loudly. It was his dad.

"Yes, papa?"

"Where are you?"

"Papa, I am here only."

"Where here?"

"I am at Dev's house"

"It is getting late, come home right now."

"Okay, papa. I'll be there in 10 minutes."

"Hmm."

Dev: "What happened, Mayank bhai?"

Mayank: "Dad, yaar. We should go home now."

Khan: "What is the time?"

Luv: "Bro, it is 10:30 PM."

Shiv: "Yeah, let's go home."

Dev: "Guys, is everyone alright? I hope everyone is fine and sober enough to go home."

Everyone: "Yes, we are."

Dev: "Even if you are not, please take my advice and go straight to your room, lie down on a soft bed and don't wake up till tomorrow afternoon. Cheers! Happy Diwali, folks."

Everyone: "HAPPY DIWALI!"

CHAPTER THIRTEEN

School had reopened. Students were happy during the first week. There wasn't much study going on at the school. Teachers were going easy too.

Prateek, Mudit and the other studious kids were busy trying to calculate their scores that they were expecting from the half yearly exams.

The D company was coming to school regularly these days, as there wasn't much work load at their classes. Khan and Luv had become best friends since Diwali. Mayank hadn't had even a sip of liquor since then. Dev hadn't been able to find a way to get closer to Gitika, and still took rounds around Study Hall, hoping to find a link. Shiv, meanwhile, was trying to find a way to help his best friend Dev in his mission.

Today was the day their class teacher was about to show all the subject copies to the students. Mudit was sitting on the first seat, waiting for the class teacher to arrive.

Anurag sir entered the class, carrying a bundle of answer-scripts of his subject, Chemistry. After being greeted well by students with full energy, he ordered everyone to settle down quickly.

Luv, Khan, Mayank, Shiv and Dev were sitting at the last bench, along with Binnu and Chikna. Dev and Mayank were telling everyone how Luv had impressed and hooked up with a hot girl in the girl's toilet.

Chikna: “Guys, listen. Sir is about to begin distributing the answer sheets.”

Dev: “Oh ho, it has been so long. We haven’t got the answer sheets.”

Mayank: “Oh, come on, dude. What’s so exciting about them? You talk as if you are going to top the class.”

Dev: “One day I will, brother. I will.”

Chikna: “Best of luck for that. For now, please bring your attention back to the classroom.”

Anurag sir took out the first answer sheet from the bundle and called out, “Ankit Singh, 52.” Ankit Singh got up at his seat and his sheet was passed over to him.

“Mudit Sinha, 84. Well done, Mudit.” His sheet was handed to him at his seat too. The guys were completely hopeless after this announcement, as Mudit, who had been rumoured to have scored more than 95 marks out of hundred and if he got just 84, which means there had been a very strict checking.

Binnu: “Mudit got only 84? What the hell, man. I don’t know how much I will get now.”

Chikna: “Yes, you are absolutely right, brother.”

“Prashant Tiwari, 69.”

“Devvrat Dixit, 4.”

Everyone in class started laughing at this.

Mayank: “You got only 4, hahahaha.”

“Mayank Verma, 2 and a half.”

Dev replied sarcastically, “Hahahaha, only 4, han?”

“Mustafa Khan, 9.”

“Shiv Shantanu Yadav, 12.”

"Luv Chaudhary, 3."

His was the last sheet and he was the last boy to get admitted in the school.

"If anyone finds any mistake in counting, and counting only, he or she can come to me right away. No corrections will be made after this class." After this, Anurag sir sat down in his comfortable chair and started calling everyone by their roll numbers.

Shiv: "Luv, you said that your exam had gone well."

Luv: "Yes, I did."

Shiv: "How come you got only three marks then? That is the lowest in the entire class."

Luv: "Bro, you are wrong. Mayank got the lowest score. I got half a mark more than him."

Dev: "That's alright, bro. I am unable to understand though, how did Khan manage 9 marks out of a hundred?"

Khan: "That's what I am unable to understand too. Oh yes, now I remember, I copied an answer from someone."

Dev: "Someone? Who someone?"

Khan: "Arrey, how would I remember that, yaar? I copied from different sources in every paper."

Shiv: "Yeah, that's right."

Mayank: "Oh, Shiv got the highest."

Luv: "Oh yes, he did."

Shiv: "Highest? Are you okay? I just got 12 marks out of hundred."

Mayank: "I mean in our group, dude."

***

The last lecture of the day was about to end. Marks for all the subjects had been shown that very day. Shiv made a chart out of the marks obtained by everyone in each subject.

	Physics	Chm	Maths	Eng. Litt	Eng. Lang	Environ-ment	Comp.
Dev	14	4	8	3	5	58	12
Luv	4	3	4	12	4	45	10
Shiv	18	12	44	54	62	67	35
Mayank	33	2.5	12	38	23	44	22
Khan	21	9	7	16	21	36	78

He analysed his weaknesses and strengths. It seemed to him that he needed to work hard in Physics, Chemistry, Computers and Maths.

Dev saw Shiv busy doing these calculations, so he went over to him and said, "What happened, brother?"

"Nothing, I was just having a look at our marks. They are quite disappointing."

"Oh dude, this was just the half-yearly. We will work hard for the finals, yaar."

"Well, I hope so."

"Why do you worry, bro? You have got sufficient marks."

"Bro, I didn't even pass in three subjects."

"And I have passed in only one subject."

"That is definitely a big reason to worry."

"What'll change with your worrying?"

"Yeah, nothing happens by worrying, but something will definitely change regarding the input we give after we start worrying."

"We definitely will," said Mayank, who had been listening so patiently up until this point. However, he couldn't control his feelings anymore and interrupted, "But, what next?"

Khan: "Next? What does that mean?"

Mayank: "It means that from tomorrow onwards, we are going to have the same old schedule. Teachers will start teaching in full flow too, since they have to finish their syllabus in time."

Shiv: "So what?"

Mayank: "Let's go somewhere. We haven't had any outing since Diwali. It has been more than 15 days."

Shiv: "No no, not at all. Let's study for some days, yaar."

Khan: "Bhai, these are the days. I mean, after a month, we'll have to start preparing for exams anyway. Extra classes will begin in two months and then the annual exams will be on our heads."

Mayank: "Yeah, exactly. Let's do something, guys. Let's go out, any place."

Dev: "I have heard a lot about this place, 'Jim Corbett Park'."

Shiv: "Yeah, it is a National Park."

Dev: "Yeah, we can have a wildlife safari and spend a night there too."

Shiv: "Dude, don't even think about going to Uttarakhand. Have you forgotten about the recent tragedy that happened there?"

Mayank: "Oh, yes. Something did happen there due to high rainfall, a cloud burst, and some landslides and all."

Khan: "Oh, yes yes, I saw it on TV. So many people got killed there and Uttarakhand was destroyed and devastated totally. Even I wouldn't suggest going there."

Shiv: "Suggest!? Nobody at my home will allow me to go there, guys. Apart from that, I insist that we should make that plan only for a weekend."

Luv: "Let's do one thing, let's go to my farmhouse. We have all the arrangements there, we can cook our own food and have a bonfire too. What do you guys say?"

Dev: "Your own a farmhouse? Where?"

Luv: "I mean, it is my father's. It is in Khargapur, near about 40 kilometres from here."

Dev: "What does your father do, dude?"

Luv: "My father is the minister of state for food and supplies."

Dev: "Really?"

Mayank: "And you hang around on a Super Splendor?"

Luv: "Actually, I wanted a pulsar 220, but since it is a very fast bike, no one at home was really to give it to me."

Mayank: "What car does your father use?"

Luv: "He uses an Ambassador."

Mayank: "I know that, dude. Apart from that official ambassador, I mean."

Luv: “Apart from that, we have many cars. About 12 Tata Safaris, 8-9 Taveras, 3 Pajeros, 6 Tata Sumos, and about 20-25 Boleros. That’s it.”

Mayank: “Why don’t you use any one of them then?”

Luv: “Bro, I don’t know how to drive a car. I am always escorted by a driver whenever I take a car with me, that’s why I don't use them.”

Mayank: “Guys, this asshole definitely needs driving lessons.”

Khan: “I will help him out with that. For now, Luv’s farmhouse party is done. And everyone can say at home that it’s Mayank’s birthday.”

Mayank: “Mayank’s birthday? Why the hell is it Mayank’s birthday every time? Tell me frankly, Khan, how many times do you give the excuse my birthday at your home?”

Khan: “Dude, it is not only you, I celebrate everyone’s birthday about 5-6 times a year.”

Mayank: “What the fuck? You really do that?”

Khan: “How else do you think I keep everyone calm at home? For each one of yours birthday gift, I take 2000 rupees from my dad too.”

Dev: “Hahahaha, I also give that excuse on a regular basis.”

Luv: “So, it is done. This weekend, at my farmhouse.”

Everyone: “Done, guys.”

***

It was the last day of the week at school. The next day being the second Saturday, it was off. Shiv was attending all the tuition classes he had registered to.

All the students who had failed in any subject were ordered to attend tuition classes for that particular subject for an hour after school. The teachers used that hour to help the students understand concepts, which was definitely a good initiative.

Shiv was attending English Literature's tuition class that day, which was taken by John sir. John Briganza was Christian by religion and hailed from Kerala. He was the teacher of English at school, but he did not take Shiv's class. He was assigned for the commerce sections.

He was giving a short summary of the play 'PYGMALION' by George Bernard Shaw, so the students could get an idea of what the book was all about.

The class continued till six in the evening. It was quite late to be staying at school and the Sun had set already.

Shiv took the driver's seat after coming out from school and started driving back home, with Rakesh on his side. He saw his phone there were three missed calls.

One from his mom, another from Dev and one from Khan. Shiv called his mom first "Yes mom"

"Where are you? Rakesh told me you were still at school."

"Mom, I had a few extra classes."

"Okay, come soon. We have to go out."

"Out? Where?"

"We have this Diwali party for all the colony members."

"What? Diwali party, now? It has been more than three weeks since Diwali."

"Oh baba, it happens like this only. It takes time for everyone to get done with all their relatives and all."

"Okay, okay, not an issue. I am driving right now. I will reach home in another ten minutes."

Shiv had crossed Munshi Pulia Chowraha by then. It was now time to call Dev. Shiv called Dev up and asked, "Hey! Ssup, bro? You called?"

"Yes, I did, to remind you that tomorrow we are all going to Luv's farmhouse. Don't make any excuses now."

"Oh yes, brother. I do remember tomorrow's plan, but I am really not in a mood to party. I don't want to talk about that right now."

"Okay. How are your classes going on?"

"Classes are good. Every teacher asks about all of you guys while taking attendance."

"Hahahaha…"

"Dude, why don't you all come to those classes too?"

"Dude, if we all come to attend those classes, there won't be any studying business there. Chuck it, yaar, we have other businesses to attend to after school."

"Oh yes, I know what kind of businesses you have. Beating some guy up, or chasing after some girl, or the…"

His car suddenly crashed into something with a loud sound.

"What the hell happened, Shiv? What was that sound, brother?"

"What the fuck, man. I knocked down a scooty, man…" said Shiv and ended the call.

Rakesh quickly exchanged seats with Shiv before anyone could see. Shiv got down from the car to see what had happened?

People had gathered around the scooty. Thankfully, the accident had taken place not far from Shiv's house and the people passing by knew his vehicle, so there wasn't much problem.

• • •

Someone's scooty had collided with his car, though. Shiv went forward to see what had happened. There was a bright pink Pep scooty lying in the middle of the road. Next to it was a girl who seemed unable to walk. She had a helmet on. Since neither of their vehicles were speeding, the girl was not hurt badly. There wasn't a single cut on her as she was full covered, wearing a black torn jeans, a light blue t-shirt and a black STUDD helmet.

Shiv went up to her and said, "I am so sorry. It was the driver…" and started giving all the excuses he could come up with.

Her scooty lay to one side. The girl got up and tried to walk, but she was unable to. It seemed as if she had sprained her leg. She started crying. Shiv helped her get up, while Rakesh picked up her scooty.

"Are you alright? Don't cry."

She opened the visor of her helmet and said in a sweet kiddish voice, "My right leg is hurting really bad, I am unable to walk."

"Don't worry, let's go to a doctor."

"I don't know you. I am not going anywhere with you."

"I live nearby in the next block, in 21/376."

"21/376, in that huge white bungalow?"

"Yes, yes that very house."

"Okay, I live in the same block too."

"Come, I will take you to a doctor."

"Okay."

Shiv helped her sit inside the car and said, "You can take off your helmet now and you needn't worry about your scooty at all. My driver will bring it along, okay?" He then instructed

Rakesh, "Rakesh, follow us on that scooty, I am going to take her to a Doctor."

"Bhaiya ji, I know…" Rakesh started, but his voice trailed off in Shiv's head as he got lost in the sight of the girl who had just taken off her helmet. Her long and silky light brown hair that dropped down to her back were glimmering like stars in the evening sky. Her face was covered with her hair, which she pulled back with her hands. Shiv noticed that she had pained her nails with a beautiful red nail paint.

It seemed to him as if God had never created a more beautiful face than hers, for she looked more beautiful than Katrina Kaif herself. Her fair face was white as milk, which now became red as she had hastily pulled the helmet off her head. Her eyes were so beautiful that her very first gaze penetrated down to the bottom of Shiv's heart.

Shiv was drawn out of his reverie and came back to the real world when she said herself, "Bhaiya ji is saying something."

"Oh, yes. Rakesh, yes, he was saying something."

"Bhaiya ji, you might not know a doctor here, but I know our doctor sahab, the place where bade sahab always goes. Let's go there. I'll lead and you follow me."

"Okay," he said, but the very next moment he figured that this doctor would definitely tell his father about this incident. He quickly added, "No, actually that Doctor uncle is out of town right now. Let's go to some other doctor."

Rakesh had an intuition that something was not right, but he kept his silence and simply followed Shiv's orders. Shiv reversed the car and started heading towards Munshi Pulia, in hope to find a doctor there.

"Shit, I shouldn't have taken out the scooty. Mom is going to kill me," said the girl in a troubled tone.

"Don't worry, you will be okay. There are only some minor scratches on your scooty. Your leg will be fine too. I just hope it is not a fracture."

"Oh no, I don't think it is a fracture. My dad had a fracture in his leg some time back, and his leg got swollen like hell. I don't have any swellings, look."

Shiv took a quick glance of her feet and said, "Oh yes, you don't have any swelling."

"It is just hurting a lot near the ankle."

"Hmm, it might be a sprain."

"So, you are Uma aunty's son, Shiv?"

"Oh yes, I am. How do you know my name?"

"Your mother mentioned you in a few conversations."

"Now don't tell me that you are my mother's friend."

"No, not me. My mom is a friend of you mom. She mentioned how her son had returned from Nainital and had joined a school here."

"Oh, that's great. It will be really nice if I too get to know the name of the beautiful girl sitting next to me and knows so much about me."

"Oh, I am so sorry. Hi, I am Tanu and I study at Study Home. I am in class 11th, commerce section."

"That's great, and as you already know, I am Shiv and I study at LMS, 11th standard too, but in science section."

"I have seen this car before and I knew it's from Uma aunty's house. That's the only reason I agreed to sit in here."

"Oh, that's great. I think I should get some doctor's address from Just Dial."

• • •

“There is no need. I actually feel quite better now. I should just get a Moov spray and get back home.”

“What? Are you sure? I mean, are you okay?”

“Yes. I think I am fine. I just shouldn’t have taken out the new scooty, since I don’t know how to ride it properly yet. I was just trying to learn when this happened. If someone at home comes to know that I got hurt, believe me, I won’t ever be allowed to touch my scooty again.”

“Hahaha, don’t worry about it. No one’s going to know anything. In case you need riding lessons, I can definitely help you with that too.”

“Really? That’s so nice of you. Do you have a licence?”

“No, not yet, but I do know how to ride a scooty, believe me.”

“I do. Now, will you please drop me back where you found me?”

“Yeah, sure. I am really very very sorry for the accident. Please accept my apologies.”

“Oh ho, it’s okay. Don't worry.”

“Oh, come on, please let me pay for the Moov spray at least.”

“It’s okay, Shiv.It’s not a problem, yaar.”

“I insist, please.”

“Here, you drop me right here. I will manage from here on.”

“Okay, I hope you get well soon.”

“Thank you, see you later, b-bye.”

“Bye.”

• • •

CHAPTER FOURTEEN

"Hey, Dev. Today's a good chance since you and I are alone and no one else is present today."

"Yes, what did you want from me in private?"

"Do you really think you have something you can give me in private?"

"Asshole, tell me, what do you want?"

"Dude, I don't want anything. I just want you to turn to Study Home."

"Study Home! Yeah yeah, sure, why not? Definitely, let's go there anytime."

Dev turned his car around towards Study Home. More than a week had passed since Shiv had befriended Tanu. They had even visited each other's place and had started hanging out together, but not even a single dude from the D-company had any idea about this.

Luv had been busy with Priyanka, and had now become a real dude in the truest sense. Khan and Dev had been giving him driving lessons and he had started using a white safari for himself, with a red beacon over it too.

"There is Study Home."

"Dude, park the car at the back gate."

“Park? Why park, buddy?”

“Just do as I say, bro.”

“Okay.”

The moment Dev turned the car to head for the back gate, he was shocked.

“Shiv bhai, look! Geetika is standing there, yaar, with another gorgeous girl.”

“Yeah, just stop the car in front of them.”

“Are you crazy, asshole? I don’t want to seem like a hooligan or a goon. I will not stop there.”

“Are baba, trust me! Just stop there.”

“Okay, as you say.”

Dev stopped there as directed by Shiv. Shiv went forward towards Tanu (the other gorgeous girl) and before he could uttered a word, she said, “I hope I am not bothering you, Shiv.”

Shiv: “No, not at all, yaar. We live in the same colony. Giving you a lift is no trouble at all.”

Tanu: “Thank you so much, Shiv. Meet my friend, Geetika.”

Shiv: “Hey, Geetika.”

Geetika: “Hi, Shiv.”

Tanu: “You know, Geetu, Shiv lives in our colony too.”

Geetika: “Okay, that’s great.”

Shiv: “Get in, girls. Let’s go home. Oh, meet my best friend, Dev.”

Tanu and Geetika: “Hi, Dev.”

Dev: “Hi, Tanu. Hi, Geetika.”

Shiv: “Actually, bro, Tanu is my friend and just now I found out that her friend Geetika lives in my block too. Tanu missed her school bus this morning so her mom asked me to drop her to school.”

Dev: “Okay, okay, so I have to drop you all?”

Shiv: “Yeah, that will be really kind of you.”

Dev: “Hahahaha, yeah sure. ‘KIND OF YOU’ Where did you get that from?”

Tanu: “So Shiv, how was your day?”

Shiv: “It wasn’t that good, but it was okay.”

Geetika: “By the way, I think I have seen Dev before.”

Dev, who was about to say something similar, was shocked to hear this from the other side. “Really? I mean, I don’t think so.”

Geetika: “No, I have definitely seen you somewhere.”

Shiv: “Try and remember! We don't have much time left, we are about to reach our colony.”

Tanu: “You must have seen him somewhere near our school.”

Dev’s mouth dropped open in awe on hearing this.

Geetika: “Yes, now I remember. I saw you at the inter-school cricket tournament.”

Dev: “Okay, yes. I was in my school team.”

Tanu: “Wow, that’s so cool.”

Shiv: “How come you didn’t noticed me? I was in the team too.”

Tanu replied sarcastically, “Look at yourself, do you really think you are very noticeable?”

Shiv: “Look who’s talking? Look at yourself first, then talk about me.”

Dev: “Oh, come on, Shiv. She’s gorgeous.”

Shiv: “Dev, you bastard. You switched sides. I am not going to leave you, asshole.”

Dev: “Who’s going to be on your side when you have such gorgeous girls in opposition?Hahahaha.”

Tanu & Geetika sniggered.

Shiv: “There’s your house, look. Finish your laughter and get going, thankless people!”

Tanu: “Oh, come on, baby. Don’t get frustrated, we were just kidding.”

Shiv: “So was I, dear.”

Geetika’s place was just next to Tanu’s, so she got down with her too.

Tanu: “Bye, Shiv. Bye, Dev. See you guys later.”

Dev & Shiv: “Bye bye, girls.”

Geetika: “Bye, Dev. It was nice meeting you.”

Dev: “The pleasure is entirely mine. Bye, take care.”

The moment both the girls entered their respective houses, Dev shouted at Shiv, “DK Bose, what the hell just happened?”

“Drive brother, drop me home.”

“I am driving to you house only, asshole. Will you please tell me now what the fuck just happened?”

“Dude, about a week ago, I met this gorgeous girl, Tanu, and we became friends. When I came to know that she is also a student at Study Home, I told her about Geetika. She turned out to be a close friend of Tanu, so we thought we would help you out, and guess what?”

"What?"

"I even asked Tanu to show Geetika a picture of you, and the good news is that she liked you too."

"Really!? THANK YOU SO MUCH, BROTHER. You are really my best buddy!"

"Oh please, don't mention it, buddy."

"You know what?"

"Now what, Dev?"

"I think I have seen this girl, Tanu, somewhere."

"Where?"

"I don't remember, but I have definitely seen her somewhere."

"Well then, let me know when you remember."

"But really, thank you so much, bro!"

***

"My father is going to kill me if I fail my annual exams," said Dev while sipping coffee at a Café Coffee Day in Indranagar.

"Bro, same is the case with me. Even my father is going to kill me," said Mayank who was also terrified of the exams that were now only two weeks away.

"We haven't even finished half of the syllabus yet," Shiv complained while blowing out a puff of his cigarette.

"Half the syllabus? Dude, when did we start to study? I haven't even read a single chapter of any subject." Dev expressed his concern regarding the results.

Mayank: "Yes, I know, but what to do now?"

Shiv: "We should start studying as much as we can."

Dev: “You know, Shiv, the three of us - Mayank, Khan and I - have never studied anything since class sixth.”

Shiv: “How the hell have you guys passed till now?”

Dev: “Dude, it’s really Bajrang Bali’s grace. Believe me, just try to understand my feelings. I have tried to study many times before. My father tried to teach me with a stick in hand too, but every time he sat with me for more than two hours, I got a fever. Since then, my father has lost all hopes on me, and my mother has been helping me get decent marks.”

Shiv: “So, what do you think we should do now?”

Dev: “Don't worry, buddy. I know what the teachers are like here. Trust me, everyone has a weak point. We just have to get to know how things go around here.”

Shiv: “You say that you haven’t studied a single word since sixth standard, then how the hell did you guys manage to pass the board exams?”

Mayank: “Well, that’s a long story, buddy. I don’t want to remember those dark nights again. Not today, at least.”

Shiv: “Okay then, what are we going to do now?”

Dev: “Let’s first make a list of all those teachers who checked our answer sheets in the half yearly exams.”

Mayank: “As far as I know, the subject teachers from other sections have checked our sheets.”

Dev: “Good. I learnt from a senior that the same ones will check our final exam sheets too.”

Shiv: “Rajan Pandey teaches us maths, so he didn’t check our copies. In fact, they were corrected by Shoaib sir, who teaches maths in B, C and H section.”

Dev: “Exactly the same way as David sir, who teaches Physics in those sections, got the copies of all the sections taught by our physics teacher.”

• • •

Shiv: “What is your point?”

Dev: “My point is simple. We should first join the coaching classes of all these teachers.”

Shiv: “What exactly do you think we will achieve by joining the coaching classes now? I mean, only two months are left before the exams.”

Dev: “We will either learn something, or find a jugaad for these exams.”

Mayank: “Can’t we somehow get the question papers beforehand?”

Dev: “That is also a way, but what will be the surety of its authenticity?”

Shiv: “Authenticity?”

Dev: “Dude, you know how in the board exams last year, someone took two lakh rupees from a friend of my brother in exchange for the question paper, but there wasn’t even a single question from that paper in the actual exam he gave.”

Shiv: “Hmm”

Dev: “Getting the question paper leaked is not ideal, I don't have a good feeling about it. I mean, it’s not in our hands. Even if we somehow manage to get the authentic question paper, we will still have to look out for the correct answers.”

Shiv: “Hmm…okay.”

Dev: “Let’s first do this…I have got word that David takes 15,000 for Physics. Shoaib sir takes the same amount too. Bajpayee, who has recently started his coaching classes, is charging only 10,000 this time. I am sure once he earns a big name, he will start charging the same amount as Anurag sir.”

Mayank: “Who is Bajpayee sir?”

Dev: "Bajpayee, that fat man with very less hair on his head. He teaches chemistry in B, C and H sections."

Shiv: "Okay, so that makes a total of 40,000 bucks per head."

Dev: "No, not yet. These are only our main subjects. I hope you are aware of the fact that they won't allow you to move to the next class unless you clearly pass in all the subjects."

Mayank: "How much money do we need to jugaad-o then, brother?"

Dev: "For English, we have to go to John."

Shiv: "Who is John?"

Mayank: "John is the most bhokaali teacher of our senior section. He teaches English in B, C and H."

Shiv: "Why did you say that he is the most bhokaali teacher of the senior section?"

Dev: "Dude, he is the man, the Principal's right hand. If he chooses someone to be a prefect, that student becomes the prefect. He has a say in each and every decision of our school."

Mayank: "How much is his fees?"

Dev: "5000 bucks."

Mayank: "Only five thousand bucks?"

Shiv: "If he is so bhokaali as you say, why the hell is his fees so low? He is definitely not into money."

Dev: "You are right, brother. He is not into money."

Mayank: "If he is not into money, how the hell are we going to get him in with us?"

Dev: "He is not into money does not mean he doesn't have any weaknesses. I have seen in him the hunger for bhokaal. He is basically a businessman. He establishes a relationship with the students whose parents are at influential positions, and then uses their influence to get his work done."

Shiv: "Okay, dude, I find this man to be exactly what we need."

Dev: "And you know what, guys, this year is the first year in our school's history when science section students are the most notorious. For all the previous batches, this tag was always given to the commerce section guys."

Mayank: "We know that. Tell me something new."

Dev: "Did you guys know, however, that John always tries to keep all the bhokaali boys with him?"

Mayank: "What does that mean?"

Dev: "I mean, we are the most bhokaali people of our school, and I have come to know from my sources that he has been taking interest in our group."

Shiv: "Who wouldn't, dude? How many 11th standard guys do you know who roam around in big vehicles with blue and red beacons, and have their pockets full of cash and the hottest chicks in town as their companions?"

Mayank: "Hahahaha, eggjactly!"

Dev: "Shut up and pay attention to what I am saying, Mayank. The last, but not the least, one is our computer teacher."

Mayank: "Bose sir?"

Dev: "We have only one problem with him."

Shiv: "What?"

Dev: "He doesn't give private tuitions."

•••

CHAPTER FIFTEEN

A white safari with a red beacon was parked in the parking lot of Sahara Plaza. Sahara Plaza was the hub of all coaching institutes in Gomtinagar. All the famous teachers from all the big schools of Lucknow had a centre there.

All their targeted teachers could be met there itself. Dev, Khan, Shiv, Mayank and Luv - all had joined Bajpayee for Chemistry, Shoaib's classes for Maths and David's for Physics. These three were available at Sahara plaza itself.

Luv: "Guys, where next?"

Dev: "We have joined Physics, Chemistry and Maths. Now, let's go to John's place. He runs his coaching from home."

Shiv: "And where is that?"

Dev: "He lives near Manoj Pandey Chowraha."

Luv: "It's nearby. Let's go, then."

Dev: "Yes, let's go."

Khan: "How much is his fees, brother?"

Dev: "He takes 5000, buddy. I hope everyone is carrying the fees amount."

Mayank: "Yes, yes, I have my hard earned money in my pocket."

Shiv: "Hard earned money?"

Mayank: “Yes, bro. I had to sell my phone and then my tab to collect the fees for all these coaching classes. What about you, Shiv? How did you manage the fees and all?”

Shiv: “I took a loan from my cousin at an interest of 5%.”

Luv: “Really? How will you return all the money back?”

Shiv: “Let’s see. I don’t think he will remember asking me back for his money, but let’s see what happens. How did you manage, Luv?”

Luv: “I just went to my mom and told her that I needed to submit the fees for my coaching classes.”

Dev: “Didn’t she question the timing? I mean, you asked for fees just a month before the exams, didn’t she get suspicious?”

Luv: “Bro, my parents don't have any expectations from me with regard to studies, so they don't really interfere much in the matters of my school.”

Dev: “Wow. That’s great, buddy.”

Luv: “I mean, I just need to pass in all the exams.”

Shiv: “And how did you manage the fees, Dev?”

Dev: “Dude, every year, Khan, Mayank and I take a fixed amount from our homes in the name of coaching fees.”

Khan: “Hahaha, this year, I took more than 80,000 bucks.”

Shiv: “Wait a minute, then why did Mayank sell his phone and his tab?”

Mayank: “Because I had already exhausted all that money with Aradhana.”

Dev: “Who had asked you to gift her costly dresses and iPods and phones and what not.”

Mayank: “You are single, dude. You won’t understand what it means to be in love, buddy.”

• • •

Dev: "Now it's your time to get shocked, buddy. I have been dating Geetika, my love, for the past one month."

Mayank, Khan and Luv: "Geetika, that Study Hall girl? Really, how did all this happen? And you didn't tell us anything about it for so long, you 'DK Bose'."

Shiv: "Guys, let's not talk about that now. Look there, do you see that yellow house across the road? That's John's house."

Dev: "Luv bhai, park the car right in front of his gate. Let him know who all have come to pay him a visit."

Luv: "Yeah, sure."

The gate was open and all five of them entered John's house. His house seemed far too big to be the house of a teacher. John had made a classroom at the back of his house, where all the students were sitting and waiting for him.

Dev opened the door of the drawing room where John was sitting with a student, explaining some text to her. Dev knocked at the door and said, "Sir, may we come in?"

Without looking up, he said, "Wait in the classroom, I will be there in a minute."

"Sir, we just wanted to talk to you for a minute."

John was quite shocked now, as he wasn't used to getting an answer back. He looked up in surprise. "Oh my God, I didn't know that I have celebrities visiting my place today, or I would have made some special arrangements for you guys."

Everyone got embarrassed at this comment. Dev showed some courage and said, "Good evening, sir."

"Good evening. You are all Kavita ma'am's students, right?"

"Yes, sir. Absolutely right, sir."

“Which section?”

“D section, sir.”

“What can I do for you boys?”

“Sir, we are all facing problems in English. We have thus come under your shelter, sir. If you could guide us…”

“Isn’t it quite late for seeking guidance?”

“That’s the only reason we have come to you, sir. Everyone knows who the best teacher is to help us pass these exams.”

“Hmm…”

“Let’s be frank, what’s your level?”

“Sir, we don’t even know a single thing. We have hardly attended more than ten lectures this year, but Shiv is the most qualified one among us. He has attended about half the lectures,” said Dev and pointed towards Shiv.

“He’s Shiv, okay. And you are?”

“Sir, I am Dev. That is Mustafa Khan. That’s Mayank Verma, and that is Luv Chaudhary.”

“Luv Chaudhary, son of Mantri ji?” John now seemed to have fallen in their trap.

“Yes sir,” replied a shy Luv.

“Someone told me in the staffroom about you. Why are you studying at all, when you know you have to join politics only?”

Luv was shocked. He hadn’t expected John to target him straightaway. “Sir, papa says that studies first, then do whatever you want,” he managed to say somehow.

“Hmm, he is absolutely right. A well-educated person can do any job much better than a non-educated one.”

“Yes, sir. You are absolutely right, sir.”

"Let's see what we can do then. I assure you all that if you spend two hours with me daily, you will at least pass in my subject."

"Thank you so much, sir."

"From today onwards."

"What, sir?"

"Two hours daily, from today onwards. Get in the class."

"Today only, sir?" Dev got worried at this statement.

"Yes, my dear."

"Okay, sir. And sir, we have brought your fees too."

"Fees isn't running away. Attend a few classes first."

***

"'(a+b)^2 = a^2 +b^2+2ab' What is so difficult to understand in this, Luv?"

"Sir, where did this 'a' come from? And what is this '2ab'?"

"This can be any integer or variable."

"Now what is an integer or variable, sir?"

"'x' is a variable and any number is an integer."

Shoaib sir was trying hard to get Luv understand this basic formula of algebra, but Luv was definitely giving him a hard time.

The guys had been attending all the coaching classes they had joined for the last three weeks and were definitely working hard to learn as much as they could before the exams. Teachers had now become frank with them, like buddies.

Khan: "Bhai, what are we going to do about Computers?"

Shiv: "Yes, man. We really need to worry about it."

Dev: "Oh yes, computers. But, right now, I am worrying about the assignments which we need to submit the day after tomorrow."

Shiv: "We have already gotten late for that."

Mayank: "For what?"

Shiv: "I mean, the deadlines for those assignments has already passed, bro."

Dev: "Buddy, you can submit an assignment only if you have one."

Khan: "These assignments, practicals and attendance together carry 25 marks."

Dev: "Ten for assignments, ten for practicals and five for attendance. Forget about the attendance, we can only consider the assignments and practicals now for the twenty marks."

Khan: "So, can we get full 20 marks in that?"

Mayank: "Practicals are not an issue. The problem is with the assignment. They are lengthier than 50 pages, man."

Dev: "When my brother was in his 11th standard, he used to get his assignments written by a guy, whom he used to pay money in return."

Mayank: "Full assignments? How much money?"

Dev: "I think he used to take 5 rupees per page, but that was about three years from now."

Khan: "Then?"

Dev: "Let me check with him. If we can find that guy, our job is done."

Shiv: "And what about Computers?"

Mayank: "That technical jargon and the java and C++ really scares me, buddy."

Dev: “He doesn’t take tuitions. How do we approach him, yaar?”

Shiv: “Let’s catch him in the school sometime.”

Mayank: “I have heard he is very irregular to school too.”

Dev: “What does he do if he doesn’t comes to school then?”

Khan: “I have heard he is a drunkard.”

Dev: “Really!”

Khan: “Why are you getting so excited?”

Dev: “Is he really a drunkard?”

Khan: “I have heard. Why?”

Dev: “In that case, we only need to get him a bottle of scotch.”

Mayank: “Hahahaha…”

Shiv: “Dev, I strongly advice against this. You have already grown so close to John, why don’t you ask him regarding Computers?”

Dev: “I think you are right. I should go to him for a solution.”

***

Dev’s phone rang. It was Mayank on the line.

“Hey, Dev.”

“Yeah, Mayank.”

“Wait for a minute.”

“Okay.”

“Guys, I have connected Dev too. Dev, Shiv, Khan and Luv are online too.”

“Okay, conference call?”

"Yes."

Dev: "Tomorrow is the first exam. I suggest we get some good night's sleep, guys."

Mayank: "How the bloody hell can you be so cool, Dev?"

Shiv: "Yeah, exactly!"

Dev: "What happened?"

Luv: "Dude, we have been running around for all the subject's coachings, but believe me, brother, GHANTA have I understood anything!"

Khan: "Hahahaha. So is the case with me, buddy. What's there to worry about?"

Shiv: "Tomorrow we have Physics, and I am sure I won't be able to do even a single numerical."

Luv: "How are we going to pass then?"

Khan: "Dev bhai, I insist that you please talk to David sir once."

Dev: "What? Khan, it's 11:30 PM. And in any case, what shall I say him? That I was getting bored so I thought we could chat for a bit?"

Khan: "No, asshole. Just call him up, put the call on conference, and I will do all the talking.No one else will speak in between."

Dev: "Are you sure you want to do this?"

Khan: "Yes, I am. Now call him, buddy."

Dev put the line on hold and dialled David's number. "Good evening, sir."

"Yes, Dev?"

"Sir, I hope I am not disturbing you."

"No, you are not. Tell me?"

"Sir, Khan wants to talk to you and he is on the line."

"Good evening, sir. Khan this side."

"Yes, Mustafa?"

"Sir, tomorrow we have your subject's paper, and you know how hard we've been working, but I am still confused regarding most of the concepts. What shall we do, sir?"

"Ohffo Khan, I thought you had something important to discuss."

"Sir, this is very important. Please do something, sir. Otherwise, we won't be able to pass the exams and will get thrown out of the school."

"Do one thing, you two. Just calm down and give your best shot tomorrow. We will see what can be done then."

"Okay, thank you, sir. Good night."

"Just remember one thing, attempt all the questions. Don't leave a single question unattempted. Fill the sheets even if you don't know anything."

"Okay, sir."

"All the best,"said David and ended the call.

Luv: "What did he mean?"

Dev: "He meant that you have to fill the answer sheets. Obviously, he is not a fool. He knows why we went to join his coaching classes. These teachers know everything, brother."

Shiv: "Yes, you are right, brother. Let's analyse one more thing. Look at Maths, Shoaib has given us 40 important questions. They will be as they are in the paper. In Chemistry too, Bajpayee has given us questions. In English, John told us to just fill the sheets too."

Dev: "So, we will be able to get good marks in these exams?"

Mayank: "I just hope so."

Luv: "Dude, I will give those 40 questions to Priyanka too. I hope nobody has a problem with that."

Khan: "No, brother. We don't have any problem with it, buddy."

Mayank: "What are we doing after the exams? We should go on a vacation. We have worked so hard for the exams, we should party even harder after they get over."

Shiv: "Bhai, I am not partying till the results get declared."

Khan: "We will have a week's holiday after the results get declared."

Dev: "Who the hell needs a holiday for a vacation?"

Mayank: "Hahahaha. You are right, brother. But what will we do till then?"

Shiv: "The Principal has strictly ordered the teachers to take extra classes for our batch, I mean, for the students who have to appear for boards next year."

Mayank: "What the fuck!? You mean. we will have to go to school even after the exams? Shit, man!"

Dev: "No one's forcing you to go to school, buddy. Chill!"

• • •

CHAPTER SIXTEEN

More than a week had passed after the exams. The answer sheets for Physics, Maths and Chemistry has been shown in the class, and as expected, Shiv was among the toppers and so was Dev, from amongst their group.

Even after having all the jugaad in the world, Luv and Mayank managed to only pass the exam, while Khan scored somewhere in the middle, as always.

Dev and Shiv were heading towards Inox Mall in Gomtinagar, along with Tanu and Geetika. They had planned a night out, which included going to Zero Degree (a famous disc in Lucknow) first and partying hard there, then spending the rest of the night at Dev's house where there was nobody for the night The next morning, everyone was to go back to their respective homes.

Geetika: "You look so happy, Shiv. Anything special?"

Shiv: "No, nothing special. It's just that Tanu's company makes me feel great, and so does yours."

Geetika: "You naughty boy."

Tanu: "We are going to the disc, aren't we, Dev?"

Dev: "Yes, we are."

Tanu: "This is not the way. Why are we heading towards my school, Dev?"

Dev: “Guys, it’s only 7 PM now. What will we do at the disc so early in the evening?”

Geetika: “Actually, he is right.”

Tanu: “So, what shall we do, guys?”

Dev: “Hey girls, have you two ever tasted beer?”

Tanu and Geetika: “Yes we have, and it tastes like hell.”

Dev: “Oh, great then.”

Tanu: “But I haven’t ever had vodka.”

Dev: “Same here, I have never had vodka either. What about you, Geetika?”

Geetika: “Ah well, no. I haven’t ever got a chance to have it. Let’s try it out, we have a chance today. What do you say, Shiv?”

Shiv: “Okay, not an issue.”

Tanu: “Today? No, guys. Not today. You know one should never drink and drive.”

Dev: “Oh, nothing is going to happen. We will just have very little.”

Geetika: “Yes, yaar. Let’s give it a try.”

Tanu: “Are you sure you want to do it?”

Geetika: “Yes, I am.”

Shiv: “Come on, yaar Tanu, let’s try it out. Nothing will happen.”

Tanu: “Are you sure nothing will happen?”

Shiv: “Yes, I am.”

Tanu: “Okay, only because you say so.”

***

Within an hour, everyone in the car was out of their senses. Dev and Geetika were sitting in the front, while Shiv and Tanu were in the rear. Tanu was quite high as she had taken vodka in a high quantity. She said in her sweet voice, “You know, Shiv?”

“Yes, my dear.”

“I have heard that everyone is forgiven one mistake. Is that true?”

“Well, it depends on what kind of mistake it is.”

“A small mistake. It wasn’t even a mistake. It was just that…”

“What happened, Tanu? Tell me frankly.”

“Nothing, yaar, nothing happened. I just don’t want to remember that moment again.”

“What happened, dear? What is it? What’s troubling you?”

“Nothing, Shiv. The past is just to learn from, it is not to be discussed. It hurts whenever it is discussed. You know, this world is very bad. I feel lucky to have you with me.”

“So am I. Even a single thought of staying away from you makes me feel very very sad.”

“I love you, Shiv.”

“I love you too, Tanu,” Shiv said and he kissed her and hugged her. They both were lost in each other’s arms.

Dev was trying hard not to look back in the rear view mirror, and was also wondering when he would have that golden opportunity for himself.

He tried concentrating on his date. He looked deep into Geetika’s eyes and said, “You know, you are looking gorgeous today.”

“Thanks, yaar.”

"When the moonlight falls on your face, it glows. The moonlight is making your face glow. May this moonlight always remain here and this night never ends, so I can look at your pretty face all my life."

"Oh, you are exaggerating now."

"No, it's true. Let's capture this amazing moment. Let's take a snap."

The moment Dev reached for his phone, it started ringing.

"Good evening, sir."

"Good evening, Dev beta. Where are you right now?"

"I am near Inox Mall, sir."

"Beta, can you and Luv come to my place?"

"Now, sir?"

"Yes, beta. It is urgent. How long do you think it will take you?"

"Sir, I am with my family. I will drop them back and then it will take me 15 minutes. I mean, a total of half an hour, not more than that, sir."

"Okay, beta," he said and hung up the phone.

Geetika: "What happened, Dev? You seem tense?"

Dev: "No, nothing. I just received an urgent call, I have to go. Hey Shiv, listen to me."

Shiv was still busy at the back seat. Seeing no response from Shiv, Dev shouted, "Hey, SHIV!"

Shiv: "Yeah, bro! What happened?"

Dev: "John just called me. He wants me and Luv to go to his place right now."

Shiv: "Why now, man?"

Dev: “No idea, bro. He didn’t say.”

Tanu: “Then?”

Shiv: “Yes bro, then?”

Dev: “Then, do one thing. I am getting down here. I will call Luv and then go to John’s place with him. You take the car and go to the disc. I will finish the job there and then join you guys directly at the disc.”

Geetika: “We can wait till you come back.”

Dev: “I don’t have any idea how long it might take. What will you do till then? You guys get going, I will catch you later. Okay?”

Shiv: “Okay then, bye.”

Dev: “Bye, dude. Bye, girls.”

***

Dev and Luv knocked at the door of John’s house.

“Why the hell has he called us here so late in the evening?”

“How would I know that, buddy?”

“Hmm.”

John opened the door himself. He was dressed in a black sherwani.

“Hello, boys.”

“Hi, sir.”

“Guys, I am so sorry to disturb you so late in the evening.”

“Not an issue at all, sir.”

“Guys, I need your help. Actually, tomorrow is the last day to submit all the corrected answer sheets to Principal ma’am and I am yet to check a lot many of those. Look at the tragedy, I also have to attend a very important wedding of a very close friend tonight."

"Okay, sir?"

"So, since I cannot trust anyone but you guys, I would like you guys to correct some answer sheets for me."

"Sir, US?" Dev and Luv were shocked to hear this.

"Yes, boys. I will give you the answers, check those sheets according to the answers and give them marks accordingly. Do the totalling too."

Luv was so shocked, he couldn't utter even a single word. Dev managed the situation and said with a naughty smile on his face, "Sure, sir. It's not an issue at all. By the way, sir, which section's copies are those?"

"Dev, these are the answer sheets of your section and of the commerce section. There is food for you guys in the kitchen, make yourselves comfortable."

"Thank you, sir."

Dev and Luv sat down on the sofa. A domestic help came in with water and some cookies. John returned to the drawing room, carrying a poly-bag.

"Here, there is a pen and the sheets in this bag."

"Okay, sir."

"So, shall I leave now?"

"Yes, sir. I will give you a call when we are finished with the job."

"Okay, God bless you."

It was difficult for Luv to control his laughter, so he busted out with it, "Hahahaha, this is so good, man!"

"Yes, Luv. It is hard to believe even for me."

"I just can't believe we are going to check our own answer sheets!"

"Not only our own, but of our whole section, as well as the commerce section."

"Let's divide all the sheets into three."

"Why three, bro?"

"Friends, enemies and neutrals."

"Okay, as you say, big boss."

"Now, I will show you how one should check the answer sheets."

Luv took out his own sheet from his class's bundle.

"Dude, just take care that you don't give yourself more than fifty five or sixty marks."

"Why, dude?"

"If the guy who failed in English in the half yearlies, gets more than seventy or eighty percent marks in the finals, it would be too much and anyone can get suspicious. We shouldn't exploit the golden opportunity that we have."

"Yes, you are right, buddy."

"We don't want to invite any trouble like that, okay? So then, you check my sheet and I will check yours."

"Okay, that is fine."

"Let me tell Shiv that it will take long."

Dev took out his phone and dialled Shiv. "Hey, buddy. Where are you?"

"Dude, I am unable to hear you, let me go out of the disc. Hold on for a second."

"So, can you hear me now?"

"Yes, buddy. Tell me."

"Bro, I will take long. I am checking our English answer sheets."

"What!? I didn't get you. Did you just say checking?"

"Yes, bro. You heard me right, but I cannot explain everything to you right now. Just tell me how much marks shall I give you?"

"Dude, give whatever you find appropriate."

"Okay, then. By the way, are you having a good time?"

"Yeah, bro. I am having fun."

"Okay then, have fun."

CHAPTER SEVENTEEN

Khan: "Dude, I am still not able to believe that our English copies were checked by you guys."

Luv: "That was the only way you could have passed, motu."

Mayank: "Hahahaha, but really, I had never thought that John could have helped us in this way."

Shiv: "Dude, no one could have expected it."

Dev: "It is all Bajrang Bali's help."

Khan: "Hey Luv, you said that you picked Dev near Zero Degree."

Luv: "Yes, dude. I did, why?"

Khan: "What on earth were you doing there, Dev? And Shiv was there with you too? What were you both doing near Zero Degree?"

Mayank: "They must have been there with that Geetika and Tanu."

Luv: "Hahahaha, yeah dude! They both must have been there with them only."

Khan: "Dev bhai, at least show us a picture of bhabhi ji now."

Dev: "Of course, buddy. Why not? Just a second."

Dev took out his phone while sipping his tea at the tea shop. He opened his phone's gallery and said, "Here, guys. There she is, your bhabhi."

Khan: "Oh my God, bhai! Bhabhi is awesome. Who is the one whom Shiv is dating?"

Dev: "Just go to the next picture."

Luv: "Look at Shiv's face, he is blushing, hahahaha."

Khan: "Bhai. this pic is not clear. Show me a clear picture of bhabhi ji."

Dev: "Dude, how can you expect that to be in my phone, buddy? A clearer picture has to be in Shiv's phone, not mine."

Khan: "Oh, come on, Shiv. Don't be so shy. At least show us a picture, buddy."

Mayank: "Bhai, please."

Shiv: "Okay, okay."

Shiv gave his phone to Mayank.

Shiv: "Happy now?"

Khan: "Yes, I am."

Mayank: "Bhai, is this Tanu? She is hot, man. But wait, I have seen her somewhere."

Khan: "Show me! You are a fool, Mayank."

Luv: "Bhai, I am also in the queue."

Khan: "Is it? I mean, is this Tanu?"

Shiv: "Yes, bhai."

Khan: "Dude, I have seen her somewhere too."

Shiv: "Oh, come on, guys! Why the hell does everyone tell me the same thing?"

Luv: “Bro, believe me, I have not seen her before, and she is absolutely stunning.”

Khan: “DK Bose, now I remember where I have seen her before. Dev, she is that MMS girl.”

Luv: “MMS girl? What the fuck? What MMS girl?”

Khan: “Guys, don’t you all remember that girl, Tanu Jain? Her MMS was circulated by her boyfriend, and it became very popular.”

Dev: “That MMS! I mean, the one from when we were in class ninth?”

Khan: “Yeah, buddy. That one.”

Mayank: “Oh, yes. Now I remember.”

Dev: “Oh fuck, man. Where has Shiv gone? Khan, you shouldn’t have told him this thing. Come along with me now.”

***

Shiv was in a state of deep shock. He had run away the moment he heard that MMS thing. Khan and Dev ran after him. Shiv locked himself inside his car.

Dev and Khan kept knocking at the door. They were trying to talk to him, but he didn’t seem to be in the mood to talk. Khan lost his temper too. He shouted, “Bro, it is an incident from her past.”

Dev tried his chance too and said, “There is nothing you could have done about it, my dear friend.”

Shiv had tears in his eyes. Dev again tried, “Dude, let us in at least. Remember we are friends.”

Shiv unlocked the door. Dev entered from one side and Khan from the other.

“No, buddy. Why the hell are you crying?” Dev tried to soothe him.

"Listen, it is an act from the past. Why the hell are you feeling so ashamed about it? It wasn't your MMS, then why are you taking it so seriously?" Khan tried again, but when Shiv didn't answered him still, he signalled at Dev to leave them alone.

Shiv was hiding his face in his hands. Khan forced his head back up by pulling him by his hair and gave him a tight slap. Shiv's face turned red immediately.

"You asshole! How dare you slap me?" Shiv punched Khan in his face.

Khan's face became red too. He caught both of Shiv's hands in his and shouted, "Did she betrayed you? Have she slept with someone else while pretending to be in love with you? Has she ditched you? No! Then why the hell are you acting like a child?"

Shiv stared at Khan with his eyes wide open.

Getting no response from Shiv still, Khan yelled at him again, "Tell me, Shiv? She didn't ditch you. It was a mistake, somebody tricked her. Somebody made her fall in love with him and used her by uploading her MMS. Try to understand her trauma, how she must have felt when this thing broke out in public. Instead of being a man and standing with her in her hour of need, you are behaving like a COWARD!"

Shiv was slowly calming down now. Khan loosened his grip over his hands, "Listen to me again, I just told you what I know. I never said that she betrayed you. Apart from all that, everyone has a past about which no one can do anything. Not me, not you, nor anyone else. Just calm your mind and be strong."

"Here, have some water. You will feel better," Khan offered after a pause.

Meanwhile, the others arrived there too.

• • •

Luv: “Hey bro, you okay now?”

Mayank: “I got terrified when he ran away.”

Dev: “So was I.”

Khan: “Nothing happened, yaar. Stop making fun of him, now. And you, Shiv, D K Bose, you punched me in the face! Do you have any idea how much this face is worth?”

Shiv: “You slapped me first, buddy.”

Khan: “You poor man. This face of mine is worth billions of rupees, brother. This face that you have punched today will become the face of Indian CINEMA one day. I will be the King of Bollywood, just as SRK.”

Mayank: “Only if you continue speaking dialogues, the way you are doing now, hahaha.”

***

“Mayank Verma, 41.”

“Saumya Singh, 81.”

“Mudit Sinha, 94.”

Bose sir was distributing the answer sheets of Computers in the last period. Only this subject’s answer sheets were left to be shown in the class. Bose sir had taken quite some time to display the answer sheets, as he had not been well.

“Mustafa Khan, 11.”

“Devvrat Dixit, 19.”

“Shiv Shantanu, 53.”

“Luv Chaudhary, 13.”

Dev: “What the fuck, man?”

Shiv: “What happened, bro?”

Dev: "Didn't you hear what the bloody hell just happened? There are only three students who have failed this subject."

Khan: "This is the only subject we have failed, brother."

Dev: "Hmm."

Mayank: "I was lucky to be sitting behind Mohit Chikna and he showed me the two programs that they had asked in the exam."

Dev: "It seems like we three are the most unlucky students of the class. If anyone at my home comes to know about it, I am screwed."

Khan: "Oh, do not talk about getting screwed, there has to be some way out. Just one subject shouldn't be the one to screw us."

Luv: "Dev bhai, I think we should talk to John."

Dev: "I was also thinking the same thing."

Dev took out his phone and messaged John about his problem.

Dev: "I have messaged him."

Khan: "You are a fool. You shouldn't have messaged him you idiot. These topics are not to be discussed over messages."

Dev: "Arrey, it's not a big deal. I just reported to him that the three of us have failed in Computes, nothing else. Look, he has replied too."

Shiv: "What does he say?"

Dev: "He has asked the three of us to go over to his place at 1600 hours."

Luv: "Do you really think something can still happen? I mean, can he do something?"

Dev: "Dude I also don't know whether he can do something or not. I just know that he has called us to his place, that's it."

Khan: "We should get there on time."

Dev: "Yes, we should."

***

There were no student at John's house that evening. A blue Maruti Esteem, which they have never seen before, was parked outside his house. It seemed to be in a very bad condition.

The main gate of his house was unlocked, so all three of them entered in. The door of the drawing room was also slightly ajar. The sound of a few people chatting was coming from inside. Khan knocked at the door.

"Yes, come in, boys. I was expecting you guys," John's voice came from the dining room.

"Okay, sir," Khan said in a low voice.

All three of them moved forward in the direction of the voice. There on one side of the Dining table John was sitting and on the other side was Bose. Luv's face regained its glow the moment he saw Bose sir sitting there.

Dev: "Good evening, sir."

John: "Dev, you sound so low. What happened, son?"

Khan: "Sir, our happiness has been ruined by Bose sir."

Bose: "By me? Why, beta? What have I done to you guys?"

Luv: "What, sir? We are the only three in the class who have failed in your subject."

John: "He is Luv Chaudhary, Bose sir. He is the son of Mantri ji."

Bose: "Okay, that's the reason he is so sharp, hahahaha."

Khan: “Sir, we will all be doomed now. How will my dear friend, Luv, become a minister one day if he fails in 11th itself?”

Bose: “Why? Oh, come on, there are so many politicians out there who aren’t even 10th pass.”

Luv: “Sir, rules have changed now. A graduation has been made mandatory for holding any office.”

Bose: “Oh…I did not know that.”

John: “Sir, stop joking. What can be done now?”

Bose: “John, nothing can be done now. Had you told me earlier that these are your students, then something could have been done. But now, I have put their marks in the sheet which I have to submit to their class teacher.”

Dev: “Sir, please do something.”

Luv: “Sir, please, please do something.”

Bose: “Oh, now if mantri ji himself is insisting, then what can I do? I will have to do something then, won’t I?”

Khan: “Sir, please do something.”

John: “What are your marks guys?”

Dev: “Sir, Luv got 13 marks, Khan got 11, and I got 19.”

John: “So sir, what do you have in mind?”

Bose: “Well one option which is coming to my mind…”

Dev: “What, sir?”

Bose: “Had these guys had any other digits, it wouldn’t have been possible, but their one’s can be converted to four’s.”

John: “Which means, ‘13’ becomes ‘43’, ’11’ becomes ’41’, and ‘19’ becomes ‘49’, hahaha. Bose sir, you are just too smart.”

Bose: "Hehehe."

John: "So, now you guys happy?"

Dev, Luv, Khan: "Thank you so much, sir."

Bose: "Okay now, John sir, I must leave. I have other appointments. Okay, see you boys."

All three: "Bye, sir."

The moment Bose left. Dev and Khan jumped up and said, "John sir, thank you so much, you just saved our neck."

"The moment I received your message, I immediately asked Bose on WhatsApp to join me for a drink. I then explained the situation to him, and he being an old friend of mine, he readily agreed."

Luv: "Sir, you just saved our neck."

John: "Now Dev, it is your responsibility to make sure that before Bose sir reaches his house, he has his bottle of blue label."

Dev: "It will be, sir."

Khan: "Yes sir, definitely."

John: "Okay, God bless you boys."

"Thank you, sir," said all three and walked out of John's house.

Khan: "YEPPIEE! Now I feel like partying."

Luv: "So do I, brother."

Khan: "Guys, frankly speaking, now is the moment! Now I feel like I can relax."

Dev: "Yes, you can say that now."

Khan: "So, where shall we go now?"

Luv: "My farm?"

Khan: “Dude, I am not talking about indoors. Let’s go somewhere out.”

Dev: “You say a word like ‘going out’ and that asshole Shiv will start shouting, ‘I have to study, I have to study’.”

Khan: “So what? Arrey, he will also agree, guys.”

Luv: “But where shall we go, I mean, which place?”

Dev: “What about Nainital?”

Khan: “Arrey guys, we will decide that later. Isn’t it such a happy moment for all of us now? I mean, we have passed in all the subjects in 11th class! Call everyone and let’s party tonight, guys.”

Luv: “Oh, yes! ‘Char baj gaye, lekin party abhi baaki hai’!”

Dev: “Oh, yes. ‘Party abhi baaki hai,’ buddy.”

Khan: “Call everyone, let’s party harder, boys.”

Before Luv could take his phone out to call Shiv and Mayank, it started ringing itself.

Luv: “Hey guys, I’ve got to take this call. Just give me a minute.”

Khan: “Darling, you can have all the time in this world, my baby.”

Dev: “Khan, stop it buddy. You are reckless.”

Khan: “Look at his face. Can you tell, Dev, whose call it is?”

Dev: “It must be his father, that’s why he has gone aside.”

Khan: “Hmm, he must be telling him that he has passed class 11th.”

Dev: “Hahahaha. So Khan, tell me…what exactly do you have in mind about a vacation?”

Khan: “Dude, I was thinking, let’s go to Delhi.”

Dev: “Dude, you know I never have an issue. It is the others who have issues, not me.”

Khan: “Look here, Luv is back.”

Luv was back, but his face didn’t have the glow he had five minutes ago. His face was completely pale and tension could clearly be seen on his forehead. His eyes were swimming with tears. Both Dev and Khan were shocked to see tears in his eyes. Khan approached him and asked, “What the hell happened, buddy? Why the tears, man? What happened, buddy?”

Dev too was horrified. The unfortunate day when Khan’s mother had passed away flashed in front of his eyes. In his heart, he started praying, ‘God, please! I don’t want to hear that kind of news again.” He found the courage to ask Luv again, “What happened, bro? Calm down.”

Luv wasn’t crying aloud, he just looked numb. A few drops of tears emerged from his eyes. He mumbled something, but he wasn’t audible.

“What? I didn’t get you, buddy,” Khan said softly.

“Bro, I am screwed up.”

“What the hell happened?”

“Dude, my father is not going to leave me. He is going to kill me, bro.”

“Bro, just tell us what the fuck happened. Maybe we can help you.”

“Bhai, Priyanka is pregnant.”

TO BE CONTINUED…

About the Author

Aditya Mishra was born in Ranchi and has since lived in different cities throughout his growing years. From St. Joseph's in Gorakhpur to St. Basil's in Basti, he made his way to Birla Vidya Mandir in Nainital and then ended up at City Montessori School, in Gomti Nagar, Lucknow. He is now an IT graduate from Amplify Mindware Bhartiya Vidyapeeth University, Pune.

He is known for his jolly and friendly nature, and has a good sense of humour, which he has tried to put in his book to the best of his capacity. He is is now pursuing higher studies. He can be reached at:

adityamishram@gmail.com
https://www.facebook.com/profile.php?id=669933423&ref=bookmarks

Printed by Libri Plureos GmbH in Hamburg,
Germany

9 789387 328594